8-279

J
BRE

Brett, Simon.

The three
detectives and the
knight in armor

$12.95   g

DATE			

The Three Detectives
and the
Knight in Armor

The Three Detectives and the Knight in Armor

SIMON BRETT

CHARLES SCRIBNER'S SONS • NEW YORK

Copyright © 1987 by Simon Brett

All rights reserved. No part of this book may be reproduced or transmitted in any form or by any means, electronic or mechanical, including photocopying, recording, or by any information storage and retrieval system, without permission in writing from the Publisher.

Charles Scribner's Sons Books for Young Readers
Macmillan Publishing Company
866 Third Avenue, New York, NY 10022
Collier Macmillan Canada, Inc.

Printed in the United States of America
First Edition
10 9 8 7 6 5 4 3 2 1

Library of Congress Cataloging-in-Publication Data
Brett, Simon.
The three detectives and the knight in armor.
Summary: Three young detectives suspect someone of trying to steal medieval suits of armor from Scalethorpe Castle.
[1. Mystery and detective stories.
2. Knights and knighthood—Fiction] I. Title.
PZ7.B756Th   1987   [Fic]   87-16566
ISBN 0-684-18895-3

For ALASTAIR,
who wanted one too

Contents

The Three Detectives
and the
Knight in Armor

1

The Knight in Armor

Stewart Hinde had been to the dentist. He had needed three fillings and his jaw still felt strange and dead from the injections. He had also got the usual lecture from the dentist about eating too many sweets and not brushing his teeth often enough. In fact, the only good thing about the visit was that it had meant some time off from school.

Not enough time, though. The appointment had been at a quarter to two and he had left the dentist's office at two-thirty. Walking quickly, he could have been back at school in ten minutes and still have more than an hour of history. But he didn't feel like walking quickly. If he dawdled, he wouldn't get back to school till after three o'clock and then he might be able to survive till freedom at a quarter to four. So he walked around the long way, through the woods.

Stewart was sorry that he found history so boring now. He'd liked it when he was younger. He liked stories set in the past and he'd enjoyed thinking back in time, trying to imagine what it must have been like to live in a different century. But his new history teacher, Mr. Hendricks, seemed determined to take all the fun out of the subject.

It was a warm spring day, and walking through the woods was pleasant, especially because Stewart had that nice, daring feeling of doing something he shouldn't be doing. He wondered how long he could make the walk back to school last.

But it was a small woods and, however much he slowed down and zigzagged, he was soon going to be out of it. Already the trees were thinning. Then he'd be on the common, and he'd actually be able to see the school from there. His little period of freedom was coming to an end.

He lingered at the edge of the common, still in the shadow of the trees, and looked back wistfully into the woods. The sun filtered through the leaves, forming little sparkling pools of light on the damp ground.

The pattern of light and darkness made him blink, and it was as he blinked that he saw it. No more than sixty feet away from him was a knight in full armor.

The knight had his back half-turned away from Stewie and was standing frozen in mid-movement, as if looking for something. A shaft of sunlight glinted on his helmet and the rounded metal of his shoulder. He was wearing full-plate armor, and his visor was down. He was small, not much taller than Stewie himself.

2

Stewie blinked again, half-believing that when he re-opened his eyes the strange sight would have disappeared.

But no. The knight was still there.

He was moving now, looking this way and that, still as if he had lost something. He turned and saw Stewie. Both froze with shock. Stewie could see nothing of the knight's face through the narrow slits of the visor.

The boy moved first. Taking a half-step forward, he asked politely, "Can I help you?"

The knight in armor drew back; then, with surprising speed for someone so heavily laden, he hurried off into the woods. There was hardly a sound as he went, except perhaps for a soft padding of footsteps on the damp ground.

"Hey! Don't go! Wait!" shouted Stewie, and he started to run after the vanishing figure.

But the knight moved fast and was soon invisible among the trees. Stewie came to a halt, panting. He listened. He could hear nothing but the rustling of leaves in the wind. He stood still for a moment, then moved slowly back toward the common and school.

As he walked along, he thought. He didn't believe in ghosts. But he hadn't imagined it. He had definitely seen a knight in full armor at the edge of the woods. It was most peculiar.

There must be an explanation. Stewie was certain that everything could be explained if you investigated it deeply enough.

He wondered . . . Was it possible that this could be a case for the Three Detectives?

3

✦ 2 ✦

The Three Detectives

It was always easiest for them to meet at Marcus's house, because he was an only child and his parents were usually away on business. Stewie's house always seemed to be full of his older brothers and his unemployed father. And at Emma's their discussions were constantly interrupted by her two-year-old stepbrother, Tommy.

Besides, it was always rather nice to be at Marcus's, because he lived in considerable comfort. His den at the top of the house was filled with all of the latest electronic equipment, and there seemed to be an unending supply of soda and snacks available from the various housekeepers who looked after him while his parents were away.

As Stewie began to tell Marcus and Emma about his strange adventure, they both snuggled down into their chairs. A spark of excitement gleamed in their eyes. The routine of school and home, endless school and home, was pretty boring; it was only when the Three Detectives had a case to solve that life really started to get interesting.

But their expressions of excitement changed as Stewie came to the end of his story.

"Is that all?" said Emma.

"Yes." It didn't sound like much when he actually described what had happened. "But you have to admit it's pretty peculiar."

"Peculiar, yes," Marcus agreed slowly. "And you're absolutely sure you saw it?"

"Absolutely."

"You didn't have gas at the dentist, did you? Because that could put you in a strange state and you might start imagining—"

"No, I didn't have gas. And it really did happen. I saw a knight in armor in the woods."

Emma shrugged. "So you saw a knight in armor in the woods. So what?"

"Well, as I say, it's peculiar. It's not something you see every day."

Emma still wasn't satisfied. "What I mean is, Stewie, that, okay, it's peculiar. But there must be some explanation for it. And, most of all, it isn't *criminal.*"

"What do you mean?"

"Well, we're only interested in investigating crimes, aren't we?"

5

"Not necessarily," said Marcus. "We can investigate anything that's strange and can't be easily explained. We can investigate anything that interests us."

"Wandering knights in armor don't interest me that much. I'd rather play tennis any day."

Marcus ignored her. It was always a good idea to ignore Emma when she was in that sort of mood. "What kind of armor was the knight wearing, Stewie?"

He knew he'd get a good answer to the question. Stewie was a bit of an expert on armor. He'd read a lot of books on the subject in the days when he had been fascinated by history.

"It was full-plate tilting armor, the kind they used for jousting. Probably made in Germany in the early sixteenth century."

"And it wasn't just someone on the way to a costume party or something like that?"

"It was a funny time of day to be going to a costume party."

"So we're back to the basic question: Why should a knight in armor be standing in the woods looking for something in the middle of a Thursday afternoon?"

"Yes. And why should he have run away when he saw me?"

"The fact that he hurried off suggests that he had something to hide, or at least that he didn't want to be seen there." Marcus turned back to Stewie. "And you didn't get any idea of who was in the suit of armor? You didn't see his face or anything?"

Stewie shook his untidy blond head. "The visor was down. He could have been anyone."

"Or *she* could have been anyone," said Emma, who was still just being difficult.

"Yes. Certainly. It could have been a woman. Anyone who fitted in the suit of armor."

"And was it a big suit or a small one?" asked Marcus.

"Small. Really quite small. Probably only an inch or so taller than me. Which is another reason why I think it was a genuine suit of armor."

"What do you mean?"

"Well, when you see suits of armor on display, a lot of them look quite small. Four hundred years ago people were generally smaller."

Marcus nodded. "And you didn't see anything through the slits of his visor?"

"No. As I say, could have been anyone in there."

"Or no one," suggested Emma.

There was a moment's uncomfortable silence before Marcus spoke. He looked thoughtful. "The trouble is, we don't have much to go on, do we? I suppose we could go back to the woods and see if there are any footprints to follow."

"I should have looked at the time, but I don't think we'd find anything now. I mean, it was damp but not muddy. And he seemed very light on his feet."

"That's odd," said Emma, interested in spite of herself.

"What's odd?"

7

"That someone dressed in full-plate armor should be light on his feet. I mean, how much would a full suit weigh?"

"Probably between seventy and eighty pounds," Stewie replied thoughtfully.

"Hard to be light on your feet carrying that much weight."

"Yes."

"And hard to move around without making quite a noise," said Marcus.

"Yes," Emma agreed, "you'd have thought there'd be quite a lot of clanking and banging around."

"But you say he didn't make any noise at all?"

"None. All I remember hearing was the wind rustling through the leaves."

They were silent. It was Emma who spoke the thought that was in all of their minds. "You don't suppose it *could* have been a ghost, do you?"

✣ 3 ✣

The Explanation

"I'm sure there's a perfectly logical explanation for it," said Marcus briskly. "Everything can be explained logically, can't it, Stewie?"

Stewie nodded slowly. That's what he'd always believed, but at that precise moment he didn't feel quite so convinced. It was the knight in armor's silence that made it so odd. A real person in a real suit of armor couldn't have moved so quickly. Real knights in armor used to be so heavy that they had to be lifted up onto their horses with pulleys. Stewie felt a little uncomfortable.

But Marcus wasn't going to join in the mood of fear and suspicion that had come over the other two. "Anyway, ghosts don't appear in the middle of the afternoon. They only come out at night. And why should a ghost want to appear in the middle of a woods in front of Stewart Hinde? What possible reason could it have for doing that?"

"You say it looked as if it had lost something?"

Stewie nodded. Emma screwed up her eyes with the effort of imagination. "Suppose it was the ghost of a knight who had been madly in love with this lady, and then he went off to the Crusades and got killed, and ever since his soul has been wandering around looking for his ladylove and—?"

"Don't be stupid, Emma!" Marcus broke in. "What a load of romantic nonsense!"

"Anyway," said Stewie, "I said the armor looked like it was sixteenth century. The last Crusade was in 1270."

"Well . . . all right, not the Crusades. He was killed in some other battle, in the Wars of the Roses, maybe, or—"

"It was not a ghost," Marcus almost shouted, "because ghosts don't exist!"

"No. That's true," Stewie agreed. But he didn't sound completely sure about it.

"People *do* see ghosts, though," Emma insisted. Now that she had caught on to the idea of being a ghosthunter rather than a detective, she was beginning to like it. "There are even supposed to be ghosts around here. There was an article recently in the local paper about it. There's supposed to be a ghost in Scalethorpe Castle down the road."

"Yes, I read that," said Marcus, dismissing the idea. "But that story's just for publicity. The people at Scalethorpe Castle are only after tourists. They just want more and more people to pay to look around and to go to all their medieval banquets and their jousting tournaments and all that stuff. A ghost—or at least a story of a ghost—is just another tourist attraction. I bet they made it up."

"According to the paper, it dates from a long time ago. It's supposed to be the ghost of Sir Roger Scalethorpe, who died, I don't know . . . fifteen something. . . ?"

"That would be the right date for the armor," said Stewie quietly.

Marcus turned on him. "Oh, really! You're as bad as Emma."

"Well, there are strange things in the world that can't be explained by all the normal rules, and maybe ghosts are among them."

"Nonsense!"

"But there have been quite recent sightings of the Scalethorpe Ghost," Emma insisted. "In the paper it said that at midnight in the castle's long gallery—"

"I bet all those sightings were invented by the Scalethorpe Castle publicity office," said Marcus.

"Maybe you're right." But Stewie still sounded unconvinced.

"Of course I'm right. There is a perfectly simple, straightforward explanation for whatever you saw."

"Oh?" said Emma. "Are you going to find it for us?"

Marcus was stung by the mockery in her voice. "Yes.

All right," he said. "I will. I'll find the explanation for you."

After the other two detectives had gone, Marcus didn't feel quite so confident. He had said he would find the explanation in a rash moment, but he hadn't any idea of where to start looking.

He was silent and thoughtful as he munched through the large supper the new housekeeper, Birgit, had prepared. It was pork chops with french fries and corn, one of his favorite meals, but he hardly noticed what he was eating.

As soon as he had finished, he went back up to his den. This was not the first time that his pride had put him in a difficult position, but he was determined not to be defeated. He would come up with an explanation for the appearance of the knight in armor. He wasn't going to go back to Emma and Stewie and admit that he had failed.

He looked at his computer. That had been useful in other investigations, but he couldn't for the life of him think how it was going to help in this case.

He sat down at his desk with a pad of paper and a pencil to make notes on possible approaches to the problem. After twenty minutes, the paper was still blank.

Marcus gave up. He slumped into a bean-bag on the floor, reached for the remote control, and switched on his television. He flicked through the channels. There was nothing on that he wanted to watch, until suddenly, from nowhere, came the explanation that he needed.

It was a commercial. "And then of course," the announcer's hearty voice gushed, "on Saturday evening it's time for more madcap adventures with those crazy people from *OOPS!*"

Marcus groaned. *OOPS!* was one of those awful programs in which people were taken to unlikely places and made to do silly things by a team of painfully cheerful hosts. His finger hovered over the "off" button.

But the next picture that came on the screen stopped him. A castle appeared, and in front of it stood a knight in armor.

"And this week," the announcer purred on, "they've been meddling with the Middle Ages at Scalethorpe Castle!"

The knight on the screen raised his visor to reveal Chris Chitty, the program's chief host; whose face was extremely well-known and presumably well-loved (though not by Marcus, who found him utterly revolting).

Chris Chitty gave a huge grin. "Yes, it's medieval mayhem, all right, this Saturday. See how those knights in armor used to eat!"

A large bearded face, a bit like Henry VIII's, appeared on the screen. It opened its mouth seconds before being covered with a custard pie.

"Oops!" cried Chris Chitty, who seemed to find this very funny. "And find out how they got punished!"

Another face flashed up. This man was trapped around the neck in a wooden pillory, with his hands held in holes on either side. An egg splattered on his forehead.

This prompted another hilarious "Oops!" from Chris Chitty. "And let me tell you, that's no yolk!" he quipped. "And then, of course, if you're a knight, this is . . . *joust* the thing!"

Two knights in full armor galloped toward each other with lances poised. Just before they met, both their saddles slipped and they fell to the ground.

"Oops!" screamed Chris Chitty in delight. "Yes, don't miss *OOPS!* this Saturday. What you'll see will be a"— he winked slyly—"*knight* to remember!"

Then he slammed down his visor and pretended to catch his finger in it. He let out a final "Oops!" as the commercial ended.

Marcus grinned. Really, this was all too easy. Without getting out of the bean-bag, he reached for the telephone and punched out a familiar number.

"Oh, hello," he said as the phone was answered. And then, unable to keep the smugness out of his voice, he asked, "Could I speak to Emma, please?"

✣ 4 ✣

Oops!

Marcus still looked smug on Saturday when he ushered Emma and Stewie into his den. It was a quarter after six. *OOPS!* was scheduled to start at six-thirty. Birgit had provided a nice little feast of Coke and snacks.

When they were all sitting comfortably facing the television, Marcus smiled triumphantly. "I said I'd find an explanation for the knight in armor, and you're about to witness that explanation."

"It may not explain it," said Emma grumpily. But she spoke without hope.

"Oh, come on! Stewie sees a knight in armor in the woods less than a mile away from Scalethorpe Castle, and then we find out that there was a television camera crew around at the castle filming lots of people in suits of armor. It seems a bit of a coincidence to me. The knight Stewie saw must have wandered away from the filming."

15

"I admit it does seem likely . . ." Emma felt that she was losing ground. "But we can't be absolutely sure."

"All we have to do to be sure is to watch *OOPS!*"

Emma made a face. "Yes. How awful. You know, my father's directing a show for the company that makes *OOPS!* He said he could get me tickets to go to a taping if I wanted to. He was joking." She thought for a moment. "At least, I hope he was joking. He ought to know my tastes by now."

"It's not my favorite program either," Marcus agreed.

"I hate shows where members of the public make fools of themselves and the hosts laugh at them."

"Shows like that are very popular. Millions and millions of people watch them every week."

"That doesn't mean that they're *good*." With a father who was a television director, Emma had strong views on the subject.

"I didn't say it did," said Marcus.

Stewie remained silent. He was the one who had actually seen the knight in armor and he had thought a lot about the strange apparition in the last few days. He was anxious to have it explained.

The watch on Marcus's wrist beeped. "A minute to go." It was typical of him to have set the alarm. He reached for the remote control, switched the television on, then pressed a couple more buttons. "I'll tape it in case there's anything we want to check." The video-recorder clicked and whirred into life.

The station break was followed by cheery music,

16

brightly colored cartoons of people falling over, and finally the word *OOPS!*

The first shot was of a row of suits of armor in an ancient stone hall. The camera moved along the still, upright figures. A giggle was heard and one of the suits of armor seemed to tremble slightly. The camera stopped its progress and moved back to the suspicious figure. Yes, it was definitely trembling. More than trembling now, it was shaking from side to side. And the giggle was much louder.

The studio audience began to laugh. Then one metal-clad arm moved up to the helmet and raised the visor to reveal the grinning face of Chris Chitty. The invisible audience burst into applause.

He continued to grin, then raised his hand to silence them.

"Hello there, and welcome from me, Chris Chitty—the naughtiest knight of them all—to Scalethorpe Castle, which is the setting for tonight's hilarious edition of the show that only goes right when it goes wrong . . ."

As he spoke, he moved toward the camera, but in doing so, he brushed against the next suit of armor. It swayed, tottered, and fell onto the floor with a huge clang. Pieces of armor scattered over the stone slabs.

Chris Chitty turned to the camera with an expression of mock horror on his face and completed his introduction with the one word, "Oops!"

The audience roared with laughter and burst into loud applause.

17

From then on the program followed its usual course. Every week was the same, really. The only thing that changed was the setting and the people who took part, and even they all seemed very similar. There is a particular kind of person who enjoys having practical jokes played on him, and people like that were the ones who appeared every week to be knocked over, tripped up, soaked with water, and have custard pies thrown at them in front of millions of viewers. They all came through these attacks wearing the same idiotic grins, determined to show the whole country what "good sports" they were.

Since the setting was Scalethorpe Castle, all of the practical jokes that week had a medieval flavor. In fact, the program was made up of just longer versions of what Marcus had seen in the commercial.

First the week's victims were introduced. Then they were sent off to get dressed in costumes of the Middle Ages and told to find their way to the banqueting hall. But, as Chris Chitty told the viewing public once the victims were out of sight, their route to the hall went through the long gallery, "where the castle's famous ghost, Sir Roger Scalethorpe, is said to walk. And when they get there, our friends may be in for one or two *surprises*!"

Hidden cameras filmed the scene in the long gallery. The victims appeared in their costumes and walked nervously along the dimly lit passage. It was nighttime, and only a little moonlight trickled through the rows of windows on either side.

Moans and clanking chains were heard. The victims quickened their pace.

Then suddenly one of the program hosts, dressed in a sheet, sprang out of a cupboard in front of them.

The victims looked genuinely terrified, but then, when the host removed his sheet, they all put on their sheepish "good sport" smiles.

The audience roared with laughter and applauded ferociously.

In the banqueting hall, there was more of the same. The victims sat at a long table dominated by a very fat man called the Master of the Revels. A jester called Merry Andrew pranced around, hitting people over the head with a balloon on a stick. Serving wenches in low-cut dresses plonked bowls of gooey stuff and jugs of wine down on the table.

Then the Master of the Revels accused Chris Chitty of committing some act of bad manners that no one else had noticed, and the still-grinning host was dragged out to be punished.

This was when the pillory appeared. It was on a wooden stand, shaped like a T, with the top part hinged over a large central hole for the head and two smaller ones for the wrists.

Two armored guards hustled Chris Chitty toward it. The Master of the Revels and Merry Andrew followed.

The guards opened the top. "Put your head in," ordered one of them.

"Why should I?" asked Chris Chitty. "What exactly's going to happen to me?"

"It's quite easy. You get locked in and then everyone throws rotten fruit and bad eggs at you."

Chris Chitty made a face of disgust. The audience thought it was very funny.

"I wonder . . .," he said. "Merry Andrew, could you show me how it's done?"

The jester came forward and demonstrated the correct position. The minute his head and hands were in place, Chris Chitty locked the lid on him. The audience roared. They knew that the host never actually got caught by any of the practical jokes.

And they roared even louder when Chris Chitty started to pelt the unfortunate jester with rotten fruit and eggs. Merry Andrew tried to keep his "good sport" smile in position, but he didn't look as if he was enjoying it one bit.

Then it was back to the banqueting hall for much throwing of food and pouring of wine over people's heads.

Then came a commercial break, during which none of the Three Detectives said anything.

The second half of the program, which had been filmed in daylight, took place in Scalethorpe Castle's tilting yard. First came a demonstration of genuine medieval jousting. Two knights with gorgeously colored coats over their armor rode on horses in matching draperies. The knights carried decorated shields and long lances, which they propped under their arms as they thundered toward each other on either side of a low brightly-colored wall. They came together with a thundering crash, the ends of their lances splintered, and one knight was thrown out of his saddle to the ground.

The real jousting was impressive, even beautiful, but it didn't last long and was quickly replaced by things more in keeping with the style of *OOPS!* There was much falling off horses, dropping lances, and getting banged over the head. After each blow the victims bounced up and gave their "good sport" smiles. The audience continued to roar with laughter.

Then came the final part of the program, in which the gallant victims were presented with something that, as Chris Chitty put it, "would make the whole thing worthwhile." All they got was a tacky gold plastic medallion to hang around their necks, presented by the entertainments manager of Scalethorpe Castle, a short rat-faced man with a false smile called Kevin Parkin. Then, after a few final custard pies and an assurance from Chris Chitty that he and the team would be back at the castle "live" for their big end-of-series Awards Special, *OOPS!* was over for another week.

Marcus used the remote control to switch off before the commercials and looked around with satisfaction at the other two detectives.

"Well," he said, "I don't think I've ever seen so many people wandering around in suits of armor in my life. Since the program was made last week, I think we can safely assume that it was one of those Stewie bumped into in the woods."

Emma made a face. "Yes, I suppose you're right. A ghost would be a much more exciting explanation, but I'm afraid it must have been one of those poor people from *OOPS!*" She looked across at Stewie. "At least that should put your mind at rest."

Stewie was silent for a moment. Then he said, "Yes, it would. Except . . ."

"Except what?"

"Except that none of the people we've just seen was wearing the suit of armor I saw in the woods."

"Oh, come on," said Marcus. "How can you be sure?"

"I do know about armor," Stewie replied quietly. "You can take my word for it, the knight I saw wasn't on that show." He gave Marcus a slightly worried smile. "So I'm afraid we still haven't got our explanation, have we?"

5

The Armory

"Oh, come on," Marcus complained, "that knight must have been involved in it somehow. I mean, the coincidence is just too strong."

"I didn't see that suit of armor in the program," Stewie insisted quietly but firmly.

"Well, maybe he was in the filming and then his part got edited out," suggested Emma.

"Yes, that's possible." Marcus was getting bored with the whole business now. He'd hoped that their viewing of *OOPS!* would have put an end to the mystery and was a bit annoyed to find it hadn't.

"All I know is," said Stewie, "that the knight I saw didn't appear on the show. And when he moved away from me, he didn't make any noise." His face was pale under his mess of straw-colored hair. He looked almost frightened.

"So you're back to thinking it might have been a ghost?"

"I don't know, Emma. All I know is that it was very peculiar and that even thinking about it makes me feel a bit odd."

Marcus spoke briskly to shake his friend out of this gloomy mood. "It must have something to do with Scalethorpe Castle. Look, when the program started, we weren't shown all the suits of armor, just half a dozen. I bet yours was farther along the line."

"Maybe." But Stewie still didn't sound his usual perky self.

Emma took charge of the situation. "There's a quick way of finding out if the armor did come from there."

"What?"

"We go to Scalethorpe Castle and look."

"How do we get in?"

"We pay. They're always advertising for people to go and visit the place. Let's do it tomorrow morning. We'll go on what they keep describing as 'A Guided Tour Back into History.'"

The Three Detectives were there before Scalethorpe Castle opened at eleven the next morning. There was already quite a line of people waiting outside the main gate, and from their conversation it was clear that most of them had come because they had seen *OOPS!* the night before. It was a demonstration of the power of television. The whole program had been like a huge free

24

advertisement for Scalethorpe Castle as a tourist attraction, and the public was responding immediately to it.

The castle itself was complete, not one of the ancient ruined ones with broken walls and crumbling towers. Though there had been a fortified building on the site since the eleventh century, only the foundations of the oldest part remained. Various structures had been built on top of these over the years, but in the nineteenth century the great-great-grandfather of the current Lord Scalethorpe had had a new castle built in the style of the eleventh century original. As a result, it looked in much better condition than its apparent age would have led one to expect.

Even so, it didn't appear to be very well looked after. Much of the cement had crumbled out from between the stone slabs of the gatehouse, and in some of the crevices moss and weeds grew. The whole place looked slightly shabby. Presumably Lord Scalethorpe didn't have enough money to keep it up better—which was why he had to open it to the public and put on all the medieval banquets and jousting matches. And cooperate with the *OOPS!* production team.

At eleven sharp the gates opened and the crowd shuffled into the castle courtyard. All the conversation around the Three Detectives was still of the previous night's program, and there were many giggles as people remembered its various disasters and embarrassments.

The three paid their entrance money and entered the courtyard. Emma looked secretly across at Stewie. His face remained pale and nervous-looking. The idea that he might have seen a ghost had shaken him more than he would admit. She hoped they would see something in the castle to put his mind at rest. Stewie was usually very cheerful, always excited about some new invention he had just designed. She didn't like seeing him in this state.

They waited in the courtyard with a little knot of other visitors until their tour guide approached. He was a red-faced, cheery man in a green blazer with the Scalethorpe coat-of-arms on its pocket. He was determined to take advantage of the castle's recent showing on television, and almost every sentence he spoke contained some reference to *OOPS!* Each time he mentioned it, most of his group of tourists giggled. The Three Detectives didn't.

They listened patiently while the guide went through a quick history of the castle's construction and pointed out the four main towers. It was all mildly interesting, but it was not what they had come for.

However, when the tour reached the long gallery, they started to listen with more attention, as the guide told the sad story of Sir Roger Scalethorpe.

"Yes," the man said, dropping his voice to a dramatic whisper, "here it is that his ghost is supposed to walk, searching for his lost ladylove . . ."

Emma nudged Marcus. "See, I wasn't so far off the truth," she whispered.

"Poor Sir Roger," the guide continued, slowly shaking his head. "He was born in 1502 and died exactly thirty years later in a tournament."

Emma was about to whisper to Stewie that that would be about the right date for the armor he had seen, but the strange nervous gleam in her friend's eye stopped her.

"And his story is a sad one . . ." The guide paused for effect. "They say that he loved a fair maiden, but their families were on opposite sides during the Wars of the Roses. His family supported the White Rose of York, while hers sided with the Red Rose of Lancaster. Then he had to travel to France, and while he was away an evil knight on the Lancastrian side told his lady that Sir Roger had been killed on his travels. Not only that, the evil knight actually forced her to marry him.

"When Sir Roger returned, he was desperately upset and he swore revenge. It was decided that the conflict should be settled by jousting. The two knights should do battle by the rules of the tournament.

"That meant that they should not fight to the death, because their lances would have padded ends. But the evil knight secretly removed the padding from his lance, and in the tournament the sharp point pierced through Sir Roger's breastplate and went straight through his heart."

Again the guide paused, confident that he was holding his audience's attention. When he restarted, his voice was even more dramatically low.

"And they say that, ever since that time, Sir Roger's ghost has walked about this castle, searching hopelessly for his lost love. And it is here, in this long gallery, when the hour of midnight strikes, that he has been most often seen."

There was a little flutter of impressed and frightened reaction from the tourist group, and, under cover of this noise, Marcus leaned forward and whispered to Emma, "What a load of absolute rubbish! I could make up a better story than that."

Emma grinned, but the grin left her face when she looked at Stewie. He was even paler, and the strange gleam was even brighter in his eyes.

After passing through some elaborately decorated state-rooms, the party was led down a spiral staircase to the armory. This, as the assembled tourists noted with much giggling, was where the *OOPS!* program had started, where Chris Chitty had first appeared.

And Marcus had been right. There was much more armor there than had been seen on the program. Along both sides of the long room rows of steel-clad figures stood behind rope barriers, which kept back the curious tourists. And against the walls displays of swords, lances, pikes, daggers, and maces were fanned out. Green-jacketed guards stood at intervals, keeping a watchful eye on the exhibits.

"What you see here," the guide announced impressively, "is one of the most valuable private collections of armor in the world. And, as you see, some of the exhibits are very old. Over here we have some wonderfully preserved examples of Viking helmets, which . . ."

As he spoke, he led the party down to the far end of the room. Emma started to follow but then noticed that

Stewie was no longer with the group. She turned and saw him standing, unmoving, in front of an armored figure against the opposite wall.

She went close and whispered his name, but he did not react.

She touched his shoulder. He felt as rigid as a piece of wood.

She looked at the suit of armor in front of him. Between the pointed steel feet stood a small sign. It read:

TILTING ARMOR OF SIR ROGER SCALETHORPE (1502-1532).

There wasn't a trace of color in Stewie's face. "That's it," he murmured. "The knight I saw in the woods was wearing that armor."

✤ 6 ✤

The Suit of Armor

What happened next happened very quickly.

The public was kept back from the displays of armor by thick purple ropes supported on gilded stands, but these wouldn't be enough to stop anyone determined to get at the exhibits. It didn't take a moment for Stewie to duck under the rope and move close to the figure of Sir Roger Scalethorpe.

"Stewie!" Emma whispered, trying to call him back without drawing attention to what he was doing.

But, the tour guide had noticed what was happening. "Hey! Get out of there!"

His voice was immediately joined by another from the opposite end of the armory. "Keep away from the exhibits, you little brat!" it shouted.

Emma turned to where the voice came from and saw a

short, familiar figure striding furiously toward them, followed by the armory guards. It was Kevin Parkin, the entertainments manager whom they had seen on *OOPS!* the day before. His ratlike face was purple with rage.

Stewie was standing very close to the suit of armor, and Emma couldn't see what he was doing, but he didn't have long to do anything because the tour guide and the entertainments manager both ducked under the ropes and seized him by the arms. They dragged him back into the center of the hall.

"What do you think you're up to?" Kevin Parkin stormed. There was no sign on his face of the smile he had managed to produce for the television cameras.

The tour guide also looked angry, though not as angry as his boss. "You hooligan!" he shouted. "What were you trying to do? Ruin the exhibits? I bet he's got an aerosol spray in his pocket, Mr. Parkin."

"Of course I haven't," said Stewie with dignity. "I wouldn't do any harm to any of this armor. It's all far too—"

"Oh, no, of course not!" Kevin Parkin's voice was ugly with sarcasm. "Wouldn't dream of it, would you? It's kids like you that have made this country such a mess! No respect for anything! All you want is to smash things up, just destroy everything!"

"That isn't true." Stewie spoke quietly. "I just wanted to see whether that suit of armor was—"

"Shut up!" the entertainments manager screamed. "Shut up! I don't want to hear your excuses!" He

31

grabbed Stewie roughly by his shirt collar. "Come on, you're going to be kicked off the premises, young man! And don't you ever dare to show your nose around here again!"

"Shall I call the police, Mr. Parkin?" asked the tour guide, moving toward the door.

"No!" Kevin Parkin snapped. The tour guide stopped. Then, more calmly, his boss repeated, "No. That won't be necessary. I'll deal with this."

Emma decided it was time to butt in. "Look, will you leave my friend alone, please? He hasn't done any harm. He only looked at the armor. He wasn't going to—"

"Shut up! I don't want to hear any more! And if you're his friend, then you can get out, too! I'm not going to have hooligans crawling all over this place. You don't realize the value of these exhibits."

"Yes, we do," said Emma quietly. "And we wouldn't dream of doing any harm to—"

"Shut up!" the entertainments manager yelled again. Then, yanking Stewie harshly by the collar, he started off toward the door. "I'm going to see you right off the premises. And you, young lady, are going to go with him!"

Emma looked questioningly at Marcus but he shook his head grimly. Emma shrugged and went with Kevin Parkin and Stewie out of the armory.

At a distance, without drawing attention to himself, Marcus followed them.

✾ 7 ✾

The Silent Armor

None of the Three Detectives said anything until they were on the bus going home. Stewie and Emma had been turned out of Scalethorpe Castle with considerable rudeness, and they were all still shocked by the violence of the entertainments manager's anger.

Emma spoke first. "What a revolting little man! You'd think we'd destroyed the entire collection, the way he went on."

"Yes," said Marcus thoughtfully. "He did seem to react a bit too much, didn't he. . . ?"

"Just a particularly filthy-tempered sort of person, I guess. Perhaps we should have explained about the ghost. . . ?"

"I don't think that would have been a good idea."

"No, but if we had said that Stewie had seen the knight in armor and been worried about . . ."

33

She didn't finish her sentence. Emma and Marcus both looked secretly at Stewie. He hadn't said anything since they had been thrown out of the castle. His face was still pale, and a strange light still gleamed in his eyes. But this time it looked different. Before, it had been a light of fear. Now it was a light of excitement.

He looked quickly at his two companions and then grinned. "Yes," he said slowly, "that Kevin Parkin did react rather violently to someone just getting close to the armor."

"He certainly got very angry," Emma agreed.

"I don't think it was just anger."

"What do you mean?"

"All that blustering. He sounded as if he'd lost control. I think he was frightened."

"Frightened?" Emma echoed.

"What, frightened of the ghost?" asked Marcus.

Stewie shook his head slowly. There was a little smile on his lips. He was completely transformed from the pale, frightened Stewie of an hour before.

"No, not frightened of the ghost. I don't even know whether there is a ghost."

"What?"

"But I do know," he announced triumphantly, "that the knight in armor I saw in the woods wasn't a ghost."

The other two sighed with relief. "How do you know?" asked Emma.

"Two reasons. One, if that story about Sir Roger

Scalethorpe's death was true, then his ghost wouldn't be seen in that suit of armor."

"Why not?"

"He's supposed to have been killed in a tournament by a lance going through his heart. That was his tournament armor, but . . ."

"There was no hole where the lance had pierced it!" Marcus completed the sentence triumphantly.

"Exactly! So either the story about Sir Roger Scalethorpe's death was just made up because it's good for publicity, or that wasn't his suit of armor."

"Right. You said you had two reasons. . . ?"

Stewie grinned at Emma. "Yes, I have. I now know why the knight in armor I saw in the woods could move so quickly and why he didn't make any noise. I thought he must be a ghost because a real suit of armor weighs so much."

"Yes?"

"But in fact he wasn't wearing a real suit of armor."

"He wasn't? But you said the one in the armory was definitely the one that you saw in the woods."

"Yes, but the one in the armory wasn't a real suit of armor."

"What?"

"That's why I wanted to get close to it. Oh, it looked real enough, but when I got close I tapped it. It wasn't made of metal."

"What was it made of?"

"Fiberglass."

"Which is very light," said Marcus, beginning to catch on to what Stewie was saying.

"Yes, very light. Anyone could move about quietly in a fiberglass suit of armor."

"So you mean it was a fake?" asked Emma. "Sir Roger Scalethorpe's armor was a fake?"

Stewie nodded. "Yes. And I wouldn't be surprised to find out that some of the other exhibits in that armory were fakes, too."

The Three Detectives looked at each other. In each pair of eyes a new spark of excitement glowed.

Emma voiced the thought in all their minds. "So maybe we *have* got something criminal to investigate, after all. . . ."

✣ 8 ✣

The Armorer

There was a long silence. All of the Three Detectives felt inwardly cheered. Ghosts were vague, unreal things to investigate, but displaying fake suits of armor had a comfortingly criminal sound to it. Someone was up to no good, and the Three Detectives were determined to find out who and why.

But when Emma spoke next, there was a note of doubt in her voice. "Why, though? Why should someone put out fake suits of armor?"

"Well, it's obvious," said Marcus. "What keeps Scalethorpe Castle going is the money from tourists. Tourists don't just want to see bare walls. They want to see 'a bit of history.' So, if you haven't got any real history to offer, you make some up. You make up a handy ghost like Sir Roger Scalethorpe, and you put out some phoney suits of armor for the public to gape at."

"You mean none of the armor's real?" asked Stewie.

"Wouldn't surprise me if it wasn't. I mean, most people wandering around that sort of place don't know the first thing about armor. They just want to have a quick glance at something that looks vaguely 'historical' and then rush off to the souvenir shop to buy their bookmarks and ashtrays with views of the castle on them."

"Hmm." Stewie didn't sound convinced. "There's a great variety of stuff there—and most of it looks genuine. If you just want to fool a few tourists, why bother to go to so much trouble?"

Marcus shrugged. "I don't know. To make it all look more real, I suppose. What do you think, Emma?"

"I'm not sure . . . What I was wondering, though, is, say all the armor on display is fake—or say even just some of it is—then what crime has been committed?"

"I don't know exactly. But it must be fraud or false pretenses or . . . I mean, to take people's money for what's supposed to be a display of genuine armor when all the time it's fake . . . well, that must be a crime, mustn't it?"

"Yes. I just wonder if there's more to it, that's all."

"Like what?"

"I don't know."

"What we need," said Stewie slowly, "is the advice of someone who really knows about armor."

"I thought you were our resident expert."

"Oh, I know a bit, Marcus. Just stuff I've picked up because I'm interested in it. But I've only read a few books. No, I'm talking about a *real* expert."

Marcus looked glum. "Well, none of us have any contacts with *real* armor experts. Do we?"

"Do you know . . ." Emma gave a little smile. "I think I might."

Douglas Cobbett, Emma's father, had recently finished directing a television series set during the Crusades. All the time he was working on it, he kept mentioning "the armorer." "A wonderful bloke, Emma love," he would say, "George Kingston. Terrific. We hired all the armor and the weapons from him—and then he made all the special pieces we needed. He's got this amazing workshop. You really ought to go and see it, love. He'd be delighted to show you around. You'd be fascinated."

And Emma, who was used to her father's enormous enthusiasm for whatever he was working on at a given moment, had thought, Oh yes, sure. Very kind to suggest it, but I'm not really *that* interested in armor and weapons. Still, I know if I wait it'll blow over and then suddenly there'll be somebody else who's caught your interest and you'll be talking about *him* all the time . . .

But now she found she was very interested in George Kingston. And her father was still delighted to make the introduction. He called that Sunday night and arranged for the Three Detectives to go to the armorer's workshop after school on the following Tuesday.

George Kingston was a small, bustling squirrel of a man with spiky ginger hair, beard and eyebrows. His workshop was a converted barn and he pranced around it with enormous enthusiasm, delighted to be able to show off the things he had made.

And he certainly had a fascinating display to show. Stewie was in seventh heaven. The walls were hung with objects that, even though he knew they weren't real, brought history alive for him. Coats of chain mail sagged beside full suits of plate armor. Shelves were piled high with protective headgear, ranging from simple Norman casques like upturned pudding basins to elaborately engraved tournament helmets with pointed visors. On the ground lay a jumble of breastplates, gauntlets, leg-pieces and brightly decorated shields.

There were also weapons. Long tapering lances, some with splendid banners, were propped in the corners of the barn beside tall pikes and halberds with vicious-looking spiked ends. Huge two-handed swords, massive battle-axes, and wickedly thin daggers stood in racks. Maces, war-hammers, and crossbows hung from hooks on the wall.

"Gosh, it's wonderful," Stewie breathed.

"Thank you," said George Kingston, and darted across to a workbench. "Look, this is what I'm working on at the moment."

He handed across a stout-looking stick from the end of which a spiked ball hung on a chain.

Stewie identified it immediately. "A chain-mace."

"Exactly." The armorer grinned. "Give you an unfair advantage in a game of conkers, don't you think?"

"Yes."

"Go on, have a swing with it."

"Oh, I probably shouldn't, should I?" But it did feel tempting.

"Of course you should, if I say so. Go on, have a bash at that on the workbench." George Kingston indicated a dull gray object the size of a human head.

"Are you sure?"

"Yes, that's only an old papier-mache mold. I don't need it. Go on."

Stewie weighed the mace in his hand, took aim, and swung. The heavy ball orbited around its stem and landed with a satisfying crunch in the middle of the head-shaped mold. Scraps of papier-mache scattered in all directions.

"Thanks," said Stewie.

"Thought you'd enjoy it. Do you want to have a go with a crossbow?" And again George Kingston darted across the room to pick up a weapon with delicately carved ivory decorations.

"I think we'd better be careful with that," said Stewie.

"Oh, sure, but I'll show you how to do it. It does work, you know." The armorer put his foot in a stirrup at the end of the crossbow and started to wind back the thick string with a small handle.

"And none of this is real?" asked Marcus.

George Kingston grinned proudly. "Not one single item. I made them all."

Emma looked around at the display. "And you hire them out?"

"That's it. For films, television, even costume parties. Sometimes I get specially commissioned to make new stuff—like for your dad's series—but then it all comes back here and is available for hire. I suppose it's a fairly unusual business, but it's fun."

"I bet it is," said Stewie. "But you must like armor to want to do it."

"Oh, yes. I've been fascinated by it since . . . well, since I was about your age, I suppose."

Stewie looked thoughtful. Here was a job he might like to do when he left school.

The armorer was satisfied with the tension on his crossbow-string. He took his foot out of the stirrup and reached across to a box of metal objects about the size of pencils. He held one up. It had flights like a dart and a square pointed head. "A bolt," he explained, as he fitted it into its groove, "also known as a quarrel. This is what gets fired in a crossbow."

Marcus winced. "Evil-looking thing."

"Yes. Pretty devastating. You had to have pretty strong armor to keep out one of these. Come on, who's going to have a go?"

Marcus shook his head. Stewie looked keen but, re-membering he'd used the chain-mace, glanced across at Emma.

"Yes, please," she said.

George Kingston put the crossbow into her hands. "You put the butt into your shoulder and aim along the shaft. Okay? Then you pull the trigger. It's just like a gun, really."

Emma raised the crossbow into its firing position. George waved the others back. "Keep well behind, please. As I said, these things are deadly."

"What shall I fire at?"

"That suit of armor over there. The gold one."

"What? But I'll destroy it."

"That's all right. It's an old one, actually, one of the first I made. And I've just been asked to dress a scene from a battlefield for a film. That means lots of dead bodies lying about, and so the more dented their armor is, the better."

Emma shrugged and sighted along the barrel of the crossbow as she had been instructed. There was a breathless silence, then the sharp click of the trigger, a fast whistling, and a clang as the bolt found its mark.

"Good shot," said George.

Emma looked at the neat hole punched in the gold breastplate and shuddered. "Ugh. It's horrible."

"As I told you, absolutely deadly."

"That armor's made of metal, isn't it?" asked Marcus, sounding very casual.

"Yes. As I say, it was one of my first. I don't use metal so much now. I still use it for decorative stuff—you know, for people who want a suit of armor to make their house look like a stately home—but not for theater or films or television."

"Why not?"

"Well, think of the poor actors. A real suit of armor can weigh between fifty and eighty pounds. And it's very

43

hot, particularly under the lights onstage or in a television studio."

"So what do you make armor of?"

"It varies. I used to use a lot of stiffened leather and felt. Now of course fiberglass has made it dead easy to mold any shape you want. It's light, easy to manage. I use it a lot."

Marcus still sounded casual as he asked his next question, but the other two detectives knew how important it was. "Have you ever been asked to make a replica of a suit of armor?"

"An exact replica—just like the real thing, you mean?"

"Yes."

"It has happened once or twice, yes. In one or two films where they want everything to be perfectly accurate. That's fairly unusual. Most film directors don't care what I come up with, so long as it looks vaguely the right period. But, for instance, I was once asked to produce a perfect copy of the suit of armor worn by Queen Elizabeth I's personal champion, George Clifford, Earl of Cumberland. It was for a movie where they wanted to get every detail right. Lovely suit of armor it is, all decorated with Tudor roses and E's—standing for Elizabeth, you see. The original suit's in the Metropolitan Museum in New York." He grinned. "The film company actually paid for me to go to America and study it. That doesn't happen very often, unfortunately."

"Do you often go and study armor?"

"Of course, Emma. I have to. I pride myself on getting it right. I can't just make up the details, you know."

"No, of course not."

"Have you ever studied the Scalethorpe Castle collection?" asked Marcus, sounding more casual than ever.

"Many times. It's one of the best in the country—possibly *the* best outside the Tower of London. I haven't actually been there for the last six months, but I do go quite often."

The Three Detectives looked at each other in puzzlement.

"And it's all all right, is it?" asked Stewie.

"All right? What do you mean?"

"I mean it's all real? There aren't any fakes?"

George Kingston looked bewildered. "Fake suits of armor?"

"Yes."

The armorer laughed. "Good heavens, no. I know every piece in the Scalethorpe Castle armory inside out. And you take my word for it—it's one of the finest collections of genuine armor in the world."

�֍ 9 ✧

Merry Andrew

Scalethorpe Castle seemed to draw the Three Detectives like a magnet. There was something odd going on there and they were determined to find out what it was. So the next Saturday morning found them cycling through Scalethorpe Park toward the castle, uncertain what they would do when they reached their destination.

"I think I'm the only one who can safely go in," said Marcus, as he freewheeled along the track. He didn't like physical exercise, but he recognized the value of having a bicycle until he was old enough to drive. It was the very latest model, a thin feather-light machine, bristling with gears and accessories.

"What do you mean?" asked Stewie, puffing along behind on a heavy old rattletrap of a bike that had no gears or brakes and had been used by all his older brothers.

"Well, that entertainments manager is going to recognize you two again, isn't he? He made enough fuss about kicking you out of the place."

"Yes, I suppose you're right."

"He'd remember Stewie, Marcus. I'm not so sure that he'd recognize me again." Emma's bicycle was midway between the other two in age and condition, three years old but with gears.

"I think he would. He shouted at you just as much, didn't he?"

"Hmm." Emma nodded.

"I don't know. It is peculiar," said Marcus, almost as though he were talking to himself. "Till we met George Kingston, we seemed to have it all sorted out; it was just a display of fakes. But now we know that none of the Scalethorpe armor is false—or at least that none of it was six months ago."

"Well, I *know* that the armor I touched was made of fiberglass," Stewie insisted doggedly.

"I believe you, don't worry. But that means it must have been added to the collection in the last six months. Why?"

"Maybe just to make the collection bigger, more interesting. . . ?"

"No, that doesn't work, Stewie. I mean, if an expert like George Kingston says it's one of the best collections in the world, then it doesn't need anything added to it, does it?"

"No, I suppose not."

"Maybe it wasn't just *added*," said Emma thoughtfully.

"What do you mean?"

"Well, maybe there was a real suit of armor there before, and the fiberglass one was put on display in its place. . . ?"

But they didn't get any further with this interesting speculation, because at that moment they came upon a man and bicycle lying tangled by the side of the path. The accident must have just happened; one of the wheels was still spinning wildly.

As they braked their own bikes, they were relieved to see that the man didn't seem to be too badly hurt and was picking himself up off the ground. He looked up glumly as they approached. "Just my luck," he said. "A flat tire. Look."

He pointed to the path where a few green pieces from a broken bottle gleamed in the sunlight.

"People just don't think, do they? I mean, I could have had a nasty injury on that." He rubbed at his knees through his jeans.

He was a young man, probably in his early twenties, with a face that would have looked friendly if it hadn't been looking so gloomy. But what made the Three Detectives glance at each other with interest was the fact that they all recognized him. They had last seen him on television, last seen him in fact with his head locked in a pillory and rotten eggs dripping over his face.

He was Merry Andrew, the jester from Scalethorpe Castle.

"This is going to make me horribly late for work. More trouble," he said miserably. Then he looked at them. "I suppose . . . it'd be too much to hope that one of you might have a repair kit with you. . . ?"

Marcus looked blank. He had no idea how to mend the tire. If anything had gone wrong with his bike, he would have just gone to the nearest phone, rung the latest housekeeper, and ordered her to come out and collect him in the car.

Stewie, whose bicycle would have fallen to pieces long ago if he hadn't learned to repair it himself, fortunately had a different approach. "Don't worry," he said, as he reached into his ancient leather saddlebag, "I'll get that mended in no time."

"Oh, thanks," said Merry Andrew. "But I'll do it, if you just lend me the kit."

"No, it's no problem." And Stewie settled down to remove the tire and inner tube from the wheel.

The other two detectives sat down on the ground with Merry Andrew.

Marcus thought a direct approach would be best. "You work at Scalethorpe Castle, don't you?" he asked.

"Yes," said Merry Andrew glumly. "Oh, I get it. You saw me on the television, did you?"

Marcus nodded.

"Great job, isn't it?" Merry Andrew's voice was heavy

with sarcasm. "Hitting people with balloons and getting bombarded with rotten eggs at the medieval banquets, getting knocked off horses . . ."

Stewie looked up from his inspection of the inner tube. "Do you actually do the jousting?"

"A bit."

"Well, surely that's fun, isn't it?"

"I suppose that's more fun than the rest of it. I always like working with horses, so I enjoy that side. The jousting itself gets a bit boring, though. It's all so rehearsed. Exactly the same every time."

"It looks exciting."

"Maybe it looks that way. Maybe my whole job looks that way. But let me tell you, it isn't. It's boring and ridiculous most of the time. Not at all how I thought I'd end up when I started in 'the business.'"

The expression alerted Emma, who knew about theatrical slang from her father. "You mean you're an actor?"

"Yes. Well, that's what I want to be. That's what I trained to be. But, as you may know, there's never that much work around for actors."

"I know."

"So, when I heard about this job, I thought, oh well, I could do it for a couple of months to fill in time. That," he concluded gloomily, "was two years ago."

"What's your real name?" asked Emma.

"Sorry. I should have introduced myself." He stretched his hand across to her. "Gary Bettleton."

"That's an unusual name," Marcus observed, "but I'm sure I've heard it somewhere before."

"Probably my brother, Michael Bettleton."

"The television journalist? The one who does all those programs where villains are unmasked live in front of the cameras?"

"That's right. Dear old Michael, always out and about, fearlessly exposing criminals on the box." Again Gary looked sorry for himself. "He's the *successful* one of the family."

"Oh, come on," said Emma encouragingly. "You'll get your big break one day."

"Hmm. Not if I go on working at Scalethorpe Castle, I won't."

"Can't you just leave?"

"Yes, I suppose I *can*. But I'm a coward. I'd rather have a horrible job than no job at all."

"Is it horrible?"

"Well, what do you think? Being a figure of fun all the time, constantly jollying along idiot members of the public? That's not what I spent three years at drama school for, you know. Besides, the company leaves something to be desired."

Marcus was instantly alert. "You mean you don't get on with the people you work with?"

"You could say that, yes."

"We met the entertainments manager the other day," said Marcus casually. "He didn't seem the most charming of people."

"That's an understatement. He's one of the nastiest pieces of work I've ever come across."

"Difficult to work for?"

"Impossible. And I wouldn't be surprised if he were a crook."

"You think he's a crook?"

"Well, I haven't got any proof. I just reckon he's up to something, but I don't know what it is."

Marcus's manner became more casual than ever. "So if you heard of someone who'd suffered at his hands, might you help them?"

"You bet I would!" said Gary Bettleton fervently.

"I wonder . . ." Marcus began.

The actor looked at him, suddenly shrewd. "What, have you got something against Kevin Parkin then?"

Marcus and Emma nodded.

"What do you want me to do?" asked Gary Bettleton.

"Could you get one of us inside the castle, just to have a look around?"

He made a face. "Oh, I don't know. I'd get into terrible trouble if anyone found out what I was up to . . ."

"Oh, go on," urged Emma, at her most persuasive.

"Well . . ." Gary still looked uncertain.

At that moment Stewie finished pumping up the mended tire. He handed the bicycle across to its owner. "There, good as new."

"Oh, bless you. Thanks," said Gary. He paused; then, with a grin, he said, "Hmm. Well, now you've done that for me, I can't really refuse, can I?"

10

Marcus Investigates

They decided that it was safest if only Marcus went into the castle. If he was discovered in there by Kevin Parkin, Gary Bettleton might get told off for allowing the boy in, but at least the entertainments manager would not make any connection with the other two visitors who had shown such a disturbing interest in Sir Roger Scalethorpe's suit of armor the previous Sunday.

"What are you hoping to see?" whispered Gary, as he led Marcus in through a small arched doorway at the back of the castle to a murky stone passage.

"I don't know. I just want to look around while there's no one here."

"Well, you'd better make it quick." Gary looked around nervously. "You shouldn't be in here. The public comes in at eleven, and it's ten-thirty now."

"Don't worry. Just a quick look and I'll be out again."

"Where are you going?"

"Down to the armory."

"Well, please be careful you don't do any damage. That stuff's incredibly valuable."

"I know. I won't do any harm. You can trust me."

The actor nodded. Then he looked at the boy curiously. "Have you and your friends any idea what Kevin Parkin's up to?"

"No. We just think it has something to do with the armor."

"Hmm. Can't think what. But you might be right."

Marcus looked at his watch. "How long before the guards go to the armory?"

"They get to their positions around eleven. It takes a bit of time before the first tour gets that far."

"Right. So, to be on the safe side, I've only got about twenty-five minutes."

Marcus set off along the dimly-lit passage.

"How're you going to get out?" Gary's voice hissed after him. "There'll soon be a lot of staff around this part of the castle, so this door won't be too safe."

"It'll be all right. Once the place is open to the public, I can just tag along with a group and nobody'll notice me."

"Okay." Marcus saw Gary nod. Then the actor turned back and the boy set off down some stone steps into the depths of Scalethorpe Castle.

And only just in time. From above him, Marcus heard

a familiarly unattractive voice shouting, "There you are, Bettleton! Where the hell have you been? You were supposed to be here at ten."

As the sounds of Merry Andrew's excuses faded away behind him, Marcus realized that he had just missed bumping into Kevin Parkin.

They did not put on the lights inside the castle until the public came in, and though it was daytime outside, only a few thin beams of light trickled into the passages and rooms through which Marcus passed. He was glad that he had put a little pencil flashlight in his pocket that morning. The dark castle was a very spooky place. Menacing shadows loomed in recesses; draped curtains hung like ominous spiderwebs above him; and the thick stone walls locked a chilling dankness into the air.

But Marcus ignored the spookiness and pressed on. For one thing, he had always spoken so pityingly about people who believed in ghosts that he refused to let the atmosphere get to him. For another, time was short. If he was to get a proper look at the armory, he would have to move fast.

He was not approaching it by the route the guided tour had followed. He was going a back way, through the part of the castle that the public did not see. He was surprised at the extent of the network of passages he went through and the dusty, untended rooms with their huge, studded wooden doors. These doors were all open, but he got the feeling that if they were shut on some prisoner, he could beat his fists against them and scream his head off but never be heard by the world outside.

The thought sent a little cold shiver down Marcus's back.

At last, almost without warning, he pushed through a pair of heavy curtains in a stone archway and found himself once again inside the armory.

In the gloom the armored figures looked fierce and menacing, as if they were about to come to life, summoned by some magic trumpet-blast to drive invaders out of their castle.

Marcus ran the feeble beam of his flashlight across the row of knights in front of him. It flickered over the dully shining surfaces of old metal, playing tricks with the shadows behind the figures so that they seemed for a second to move.

Marcus shuddered. Then, telling himself not to be stupid, he moved forward to examine the armor more closely.

It was then he heard the sound of approaching footsteps.

Two people were coming down the stone steps from the main entrance to the armory, and they sounded horribly close. Marcus instantly switched off his flashlight and groped back into the darkness for a place to hide. If the light were switched on while he was still in sight, he was finished. Behind the outline of an awesomely spiky suit of armor he saw the vague shape of a curtain, and he reached toward it.

The curtain covered a tiny alcove, just a little indentation in the wall. Marcus, wishing he was not so fat, pressed himself against the cold stone and tried to control his panting breath.

He had only just made it. At that moment light glowed through the thick purple fabric of the curtain and he heard the footsteps coming nearer.

There were two people, both men from the sounds of their movement. One pair of footsteps moved regularly, the heels making little clicks on the stone floor with each step. The other was less even, and every other step one foot came down with a heavy thump. There was also a scraping sound of something that could have been a stick, suggesting that the second man walked with a limp.

The two men were coming straight toward the suit of armor behind which Marcus was hidden. Only a couple of yards away from him, the sounds stopped. He moved his face as near to the musty fabric of the curtain as he dared but could see nothing. He held his breath, certain that the newcomers must be able to hear the fierce pounding of his heart.

One of the men identified himself as soon as he opened his mouth. It was the voice Marcus had heard only minutes before telling off Gary Bettleton. Kevin Parkin.

But his voice had a new quality in it now, a kind of softening, an oiliness, an ingratiating sound, as if he very much wanted to impress his companion, as he said, "These'll be the next ones."

"Fine. I'll leave the details to you, as ever."

The second voice couldn't have been more different. Much deeper, much older, and with that exaggerated cultivated sound that so many politicians manage to get into their voices.

"Thank you," said Kevin Parkin, with too much gratitude.

"When's it going to be done?"

"On the Thursday night. Midnight."

"Sounds fine."

"Yes. That's when the ghost will walk again."

"No problems, I hope, Parkin?"

"None at all. The ghost'd frighten away any snoopers. Not that there'll be any, anyway."

"Excellent. You're doing a good job. I'll see you're properly rewarded."

"Thank you." Again, the humble gratitude sounded excessive.

"And you're sure no one on the castle staff is suspicious?"

"I don't think so. I think we're all right. Mind you, I don't trust that actor . . ."

"Actor?"

"The one who plays Merry Andrew."

"Ah."

"He's always snooping around."

"Well, if you do have any trouble, you must put a stop to it. This just mustn't get out."

"Don't worry. Our secret will be safe."

"Even if violence has to be used . . ."

"Leave that side of it to me."

"I will. Good. And it'll be done on the Thursday?"

"That's it."

"When Lord Scalethorpe is out of the country." There was an unpleasant note of laughter in the older man's voice.

"Exactly."

"Yes. Because it's very important that Lord Scalethorpe never find out about this, isn't it?"

"Very important."

Kevin Parkin snickered. A deep laugh from his companion joined the sound. Apparently what they had just said had been a very good joke.

But not a particularly nice joke. Marcus could hear an edge of evil in the laughter that grew softer as their footsteps went back the way they had come.

✤ 11 ✤

Lord Scalethorpe Departs

Marcus didn't get a chance to look more closely at the display in the armory. He was about to emerge from his hiding place after the departure of Kevin Parkin and the mystery man when he heard the guards arriving and froze back into his alcove.

The guards chatted away about sports and the previous night's television. They sounded amiable, but somehow Marcus didn't want to have to come out of hiding and throw himself on their mercy.

Then he heard a cry of "Look out, here comes the first bunch of wallies!", which was the disrespectful way in which the guards greeted the castle's visitors, and they stopped chatting. Soon after came the sound of many feet approaching down the stone steps, and above this could be heard the voice of the tour guide, making exactly the same observations and jokes as he had on the previous Sunday.

Marcus waited until the guide began talking about Sir Roger Scalethorpe. Then, reckoning that everyone would have their backs to him as they looked at the small suit of armor, Marcus took a deep breath and sidled out from behind the curtain.

Fortunately, he had judged it right. The tourists were all looking at the armor of the supposed ghost, and the guards were all looking at the tourists. Marcus moved swiftly and silently across to the group and joined the fringes of it, as though he had been there all the time.

He tagged along for the rest of the tour, seeing the parts of the castle that they had missed when Stewie and Emma had been thrown out the previous Sunday. Then, as the group reached the gatehouse again and most of the tourists shuffled off to the souvenir shop, Marcus walked out under the great portcullis and went to join the other two detectives who were waiting with their bicycles under a large oak tree in the park.

"Did you find out anything?" asked Emma eagerly, as Marcus approached.

"Well, yes and no. There's certainly something strange going on. And Kevin Parkin is involved in it up to his neck. But precisely what's going on, I don't know." And he gave the other two a quick summary of his visit to the castle.

When he had finished, Emma shuddered. "I don't like that part about using violence if necessary."

"No. I think we're up against a pretty unpleasant bunch."

"But what is the *crime*?" asked Stewie in a voice of frustration. "We know something peculiar's going on, but we're no nearer to knowing exactly what or how it ties in with the knight in armor I saw in the woods."

"No." Emma looked thoughtful. "And you didn't even get a glimpse of the other man, Marcus?"

"Not a peep. The curtain was very thick."

"And you've never heard the voice before?"

Marcus shook his head. "I've heard lots like it. He talked the way politicians do when they're being interviewed. But I've never heard that particular voice, no."

"But from what you say there's no doubt they were planning something criminal. . . ?"

"No doubt at all."

"And it's something that they definitely don't want Lord Scalethorpe to know about."

"No. They're going to do it when he's out of the country."

"Next Thursday," said Stewie.

"Well, no, you see, we don't know that. They said on *the* Thursday. That could be any Thursday. It depends what week they're talking about."

"Hmm. I wish we knew exactly when." There was a stubborn line of annoyance across Emma's brow.

"Why?" asked Marcus, though he thought he probably knew the answer to his question.

"Because," Emma replied, "when Kevin Parkin and his chums do commit this crime, whatever it is, the Three Detectives are going to be inside Scalethorpe Castle as witnesses. Aren't we?"

Stewie and Emma went to the same school. On Monday morning he rushed up to her in the playground, brandishing a page from a newspaper. "Look," he cried. "From today's *Daily Telegraph*." The photograph at which his grubby finger pointed was of a gray-haired man with thick black eyebrows, waving out of the back of a chauffeur-driven car.

Emma read the text beneath the photograph. "Lord Scalethorpe is pictured leaving for a week's tour of America, hoping to raise finance from American investors to save some of this country's art treasures. 'We constantly hear,' he said, 'of British treasures being sold abroad, but I am sure there are people in the States who want them to stay here as much as we do. Americans enjoy our rich cultural heritage when they come here on vacation, and I am sure there are wealthy Americans who would be prepared to contribute toward the preservation of that heritage. And I'm going to do my best to find those people. It's a disgrace the way we keep losing our best paintings and antiques to foreign buyers.'

"Asked about his much-publicized difficulties in maintaining his own heritage, Scalethorpe Castle, Lord Scalethorpe denied rumors that he might have to sell off the famous building. 'I hope that won't be necessary. Things look a lot brighter than they did last year. The estate is under new, dynamic management, and I hope that our troubles will soon be over.'"

"Hmm," said Emma, when she had finished reading. "If Kevin Parkin is typical of the 'new, dynamic management,' I should think Lord Scalethorpe's problems are only just beginning. I mean, the crime they're planning must be against Lord Scalethorpe himself . . . why else do they wait until he's out of the country?"

"Yes, but you see what else this means, don't you?" said Stewie. "If he flew off yesterday, and he's only going to be away for a week. . . ?"

"It must mean that whatever crime it is that's being planned is going to take place this Thursday."

"Yes, so it's this Thursday that we're going to have to get inside Scalethorpe Castle again to see what happens."

✤ 12 ✤

Plans

"I don't know," said Gary Bettleton. "I just don't know."

They were sitting in the front room of his little cottage. He had seemed glad enough to see them when they arrived on Sunday evening, had rooted out a bottle of flat Coke and a package of broken cookies for them, but now they had mentioned the purpose of their visit, he seemed unsure.

"But come on," insisted Emma, "you said yourself that you wanted to know what Kevin Parkin's up to."

"Yes, but—"

"And now we at least know when he's going to be up to it, even though we don't know what it is he's going to be up to."

"It's dangerous, though," objected Gary. "It's dangerous for at least two reasons."

"What reasons?"

"For a start, Emma, there's the danger to me. You know that my relations with Kevin are pretty bad at the moment. If he found me snooping on him, I'd be out of a job before you could snap your fingers."

"But you've said you hate the job, anyway."

"Yes, but, you know, I do get paid. I'm buying this place, and that's costing me a lot. Anyway, I hate being out of work. When I'd just finished drama school, I spent six months sitting by the telephone, waiting for someone to call with an offer of work. Nobody did. It got me down. I just lost all confidence in myself. I don't want to get into that situation again."

"On the other hand," said Emma gently, "if you don't get out of Scalethorpe Castle, you're never going to get the big break into acting that you've been hoping for."

"No. . . ," Gary agreed thoughtfully.

"Anyway," Marcus reassured him, "if we get this right, nobody will ever find out that you were involved. Come on, you know that castle inside out. There must be places where we could hide and see what goes on in the armory without anyone seeing us."

"Oh yes, sure. There are plenty of places. But the risk to my job is only one of the dangers. There's also a risk to all of you."

"What do you mean?" asked Emma.

"Marcus has told you what he overheard. This bunch we're up against isn't worried about using violence. If we were discovered spying on them, I don't think the fact that you three are young would stop them from getting very nasty."

"We're prepared to take that risk."

"Hmm." The actor looked confused. He wasn't, Emma had decided on their first meeting, a very strong personality. He needed people to make decisions for him.

"Gary," she began softly, "you told us you'd be prepared to help anyone against Kevin Parkin . . ."

"Yes, I know I did, but—"

"And what he's going to do is obviously illegal. He must be stopped. I mean, it sounds as if Lord Scalethorpe is the one who's going to suffer in all this. Do you know him?"

"I've met him around."

"What's he like?"

"Seems a nice enough old boy."

"Well, look, you know he's nearly had to sell the castle. What Kevin and his gang are planning must be some kind of robbery from the place. If the robbery takes place, maybe Lord Scalethorpe won't be able to keep the castle."

"Hmm."

"And if that happened, how'd you feel, knowing that you had had the opportunity of getting the criminals brought to justice. . . ?"

Her arguments were too much for Gary. "Well, all right, I'll help you. But"—he held up a cautionary finger—"it's on the understanding that you do exactly what

I say. I don't want you trying any heroics of your own. I'll get you into a place where you can see what's going on in the armory, but it's just going to be watching, okay? No attempts to tackle the villains yourselves."

"All right."

"You've got to promise me that."

"We promise."

"Right." Now he had made the decision to help them, Gary seemed much more positive and confident. If only he could get the same kind of decisiveness into his working life, Emma reckoned, his acting career might take off as well. He just needed to believe in himself.

"How are we going to get into the castle?" asked Marcus excitedly. "Are you working there late on Thursday?"

"No, I only work late when they have one of the big medieval banquets on. Sometimes in the summer the jousting goes on late, too."

"When are you jousting next?" asked Stewie. "I'd really love to see it." Jousting fitted in with his ideas of what history should be.

"There's a tournament a week from Saturday," Gary replied. "I'll get you in to see it, if you like."

"Great."

"But this Thursday is a more immediate problem," Marcus insisted.

"Yes. Sorry. As I say, I'm not working late on Thursday. Just the normal ten to six."

"What do you do when you're not jousting or prancing around as Merry Andrew?" asked Emma.

"Oh, I'm just a general nobody. All the boring jobs that nobody else wants to do, I get saddled with. Looking after the horses I enjoy, but I also have to do all the moving around of furniture, sweeping up, dusting the exhibits . . ."

"You've got to get out of this job, don't you?"

"Yes." Gary still sounded very positive. Working with the Three Detectives was giving him confidence.

"So what's going to be best?" asked Marcus, trying to keep the conversation on the subject. "If we get into the castle during the day and stay hidden inside when the place closes. . . ?"

"No, that's unnecessarily risky. Look, I've got my own key to the back door. I think it'll be best if we all get in that way late in the evening."

"Is that the door you let me in through?"

"That's right, Marcus, yes. It's the staff entrance."

"And you're sure there won't be anyone around?"

"Not at that time of night, no. Everyone knocks off at six on a normal day." He paused. "Unless, of course, there are other members of the staff helping Kevin."

They were all silent for a moment. He had reminded them of the dangers they were risking by breaking into the castle. They didn't know how many people they would face when they got inside. All they did know was that the people they might meet were not afraid to use violence.

"And where will be the best place to see into the armory from?" asked Marcus, moving the conversation briskly on before anyone had time to get cold feet.

"There's a little sort of balcony up one end."

"Yes, I noticed it when I was in there."

"There are some spotlights up there that focus down on the major exhibits, but otherwise it's empty and curtained off. Nobody'd see us."

"And do we have to go through the armory to get there?"

"No, that's what's good about it. In fact, the entrance is on the floor above the armory itself. From the back door we just go up some stairs, along a couple of passages, through the long gallery, and we're there."

There was a chilly note in Stewie's voice as he asked, "Is that the long gallery where Sir Roger Scalethorpe's ghost is supposed to walk?"

"Yes," Gary replied quickly, not wanting to linger on the subject, "that's the one."

"And it's at midnight that the ghost's supposed to walk, isn't it?" Stewie persisted.

"Yes, it is."

"But, Stewie," said Marcus, "you now know there's no such thing as that ghost. I mean, you've seen the armor, haven't you? You now know the whole thing was just made up for publicity, don't you?"

"Yes," Stewie replied. "Yes, of course I know that."

But his voice didn't sound as certain as his words. And once again there was a pale gleam of fear in his eyes.

❋ 13 ❋

Scalethorpe Castle
at Midnight

Thursday night was a wild one. Heavy storm clouds had been packing up in the sky all day. There had been flurries of slate-gray rain, sudden rushes of fierce wind ripping the leaves off the trees, but these seemed to be only preliminaries, little warnings that there was worse weather to come. By ten-thirty the night was looming and oppressive. It needed a thunderstorm to clear its system.

As they made their way toward the park, each of the Three Detectives, in his or her own way, regretted the decision to enter Scalethorpe Castle that night. As the dark bulk of the building grew larger and larger against the unsettled charcoal sky, each one thought of the possible dangers into which they were walking. And each was tempted to turn back, to dismiss the whole idea.

71

Into each mind the same cowardly thought came: "So Kevin Parkin and his limping accomplice are going to commit a crime tonight . . . so who cares?"

And into each mind also—even into the very sensible and unemotional mind of Marcus—came the thought of Sir Roger Scalethorpe. Each one remembered the story of his life and death, and, in the encroaching darkness of Scalethorpe Park, that story seemed more real, less likely to have been made up by the castle's publicity department.

And into each mind came the recollection that the ghost was supposed to walk at midnight.

They felt better when they all met up with Gary Bettleton under a tall oak tree directly in front of the closed castle gates. There is always strength in numbers, and nothing seems quite so frightening when you've got friends with whom to share the fear.

Also, the fact that Gary Bettleton was at least as nervous as they were seemed to help. "I nearly phoned you this afternoon to call the whole thing off," he admitted. "It really does seem a crazy thing to be doing."

"Yes, I'm sure we've all had cold feet about it a few times over the last twenty-four hours," Marcus agreed.

Gary looked hopeful. "It's still not too late. We can call it off now. We don't have to do it."

"No," said Emma firmly. "Having got this far, we're going to go through with it."

They all looked up at the castle. They were now so

close that its huge bulk seemed to blot out the whole sky. There was not a single light showing to relieve the deep blackness of its outline.

Gary took a deep breath. "Okay then. If you're sure. Off we go."

His key let them through the back door from the darkness of the night into the different darkness of the castle interior. The most striking thing when the door had been pushed shut was the sudden silence. Outside the wind had been moaning, fluttering, and sighing through the trees, but inside there was an unnatural stillness.

Gary held a pencil flashlight cupped in his hand, and its little light glowed reddish through his fingers. It was enough to illuminate the four pale faces, which, above the dark clothes that they had agreed to wear, looked disembodied, as if four ghostly heads were floating above the ground.

"I've got a flashlight, too," Stewie whispered. "Shall I—?"

"No," Gary's voice hissed back. "The less light the better. And the less talking, the better. Just keep quiet and follow me."

They did as he told them. As they moved off, Marcus pressed the light button on his watch and checked the time. Twenty-five to twelve. Very soon they would know the secret of Scalethorpe Castle.

Marcus had found the empty rooms of the castle

spooky when he walked through them the previous Saturday, but that had been in the morning, and somehow the feeling that he could rush out into the daylight had eased his fears. Now, with the wild night outside, he had no such comfort. He could tell, from the shallow sounds of their breathing, that the anxiety was getting through to the other two detectives as well.

Gary still covered his flashlight with his hand, and its tiny glow had a strange, distorting effect on the walls and arches as they passed. Shadowy shapes reared up abruptly in the darkness and vanished just as suddenly. The soft padding of their footsteps sounded unnaturally loud.

But that was the only sound in the dense, fog-like silence of the castle. Whatever it was that Kevin Parkin was planning, he was either in another part of the building or was working very quietly.

"Ssh." Though it was said very softly, the sound seemed to tear jaggedly through the darkness, as Gary stopped for a moment and let the Three Detectives gather closely around him.

"Listen," he murmured. "Through there"—he indicated an old door with a pointed top and a crisscross pattern of metal studs—"is the long gallery. Near the end of it is the doorway that leads to where we're going. But the trouble is the gallery's got windows on either side, so I'm going to switch the flashlight off, in case it can be seen from outside. Okay? We should get a bit of light through the windows, even on a night like this. And

74

keep your heads down . . . otherwise our silhouettes may be seen.''

The Three Detectives nodded silently and almost unseen in the darkness. Gary Bettleton put one hand on the metal ring of the doorhandle and, with the other, switched off his flashlight.

Though the light the flashlight had given was feeble, without it the darkness seemed impenetrably deep. They felt as if they were suddenly smothered in sheets of black velvet.

The tiny creak of the door as it opened sounded like a pistol shot to them. They all stood still for a moment in the open doorway, while their eyes got used to the different darkness of the long gallery.

After a few seconds they could see its outlines, see the long rows of stone pillars on either side that framed the windows, see the dark cupboards and bulky curtains that offered hiding-places for unknown terrors. It did not seem to be the same room in which the idiot members of the public in *OOPS!* had been teased, or in which the tour guide had related the story of Sir Roger Scalethorpe. It now seemed an enchanted cave, a home of black magic and evil.

Gary Bettleton moved softly forward, bending low, so that his outline would not be seen against the windows, and the Three Detectives, each one shivery with fear, followed him. Their spines tingled as they progressed slowly, slowly along the gallery.

75

But nothing happened. There were still no sounds but the swish of their footsteps on the wooden floor. None of the misshapen shadows came to life. None of the cupboards opened to release nameless horrors.

Just before the end of the gallery, there was a low studded door off to the right. Gary gestured toward it, and the Three Detectives followed him.

It opened with another creak that sounded outrageously loud, but again no sounds of discovery followed the noise. Gary pushed the door open, ushered the Three Detectives through, and closed it softly behind them.

The darkness was once again total. They could sense they were in an enclosed space. Curtains brushed against them, and Stewie could feel the cold metal of what he reckoned must be a spotlight stand.

They had reached their destination. They were standing in the balcony above the armory.

Gary didn't switch his flashlight back on. And none of them spoke. They all knew where they were. And they knew that, if Kevin Parkin followed the plan Marcus had overheard, they were very close to the criminals.

Marcus once again pressed the light button on his watch. Only a minute to midnight. As if to confirm this, from somewhere deep down in the castle, shockingly loud in the stillness, came the heavy boom of a clock striking.

It had sounded six of its twelve strokes when suddenly light was switched on in the void beyond the balcony.

Blinking in the unexpected glare, Gary Bettleton and the Three Detectives peered down through chinks in the curtains into the armory itself.

14

The Secret of the Armory

They could all see clearly what was happening. The full armory lights had been switched on, and the display of suits of armor looked just as it did to greet the daily tours of visitors. There were no windows down there, so the crooks were not worried about the light being seen from outside the castle.

"Okay. Bring it in here." The words were spoken in Kevin Parkin's distinctive whine. He made no attempt to keep his voice down. He felt safe; the possibility of being spied on at midnight inside the castle had not occurred to him.

The Three Detectives and Gary Bettleton saw the entertainments manager move impatiently to the center of the armory. From where they watched, he looked even shorter than usual.

But his temper sounded much as ever. "Come on! Hurry up, hurry up!" he said testily.

"All right, all right. It's heavy," came a protesting growl from out of sight somewhere down below.

"We're doing our best," another invisible growl complained.

Then the owners of the two new voices appeared. A curtain in one of the alcoves billowed out as a large object was pushed through, and as it swung back it revealed two large men in T-shirts, dragging in a large trolley with a wooden crate on top.

Gary Bettleton drew in his breath sharply, and Emma looked curiously at him. The light from the armory only glanced across his face, but it was clear from his expression that he recognized the two men with the trolley. Still, this wasn't the moment to ask who they were. The watchers had to keep silent; their enemies were very close.

"Right. Over here. Come on, get on with it." Kevin Parkin still sounded bad-tempered. He moved restlessly from side to side. He was ill at ease and wanted the job finished as quickly as possible.

The two T-shirted men, still grumbling, followed his instructions and manhandled their trolley over to a position in front of two suits of armor. Stewie, the expert on the subject, knew that they were fifteenth-century Gothic armors, made in Italy and weighing about sixty pounds each.

"Don, you take this lot off the stand," Kevin ordered. "And, Stan, you open the crate."

79

With bad grace, the two men did as they were told. The one called Stan went across to one of the display figures and started to remove the beautifully-fitted Italian armor. The buckles and straps that secured it around the back were clearly stiff and difficult, and he swore as he tried to work them free.

His mate took a crowbar to the top of the crate and eased it upward. The Three Detectives watched, hardly daring to breathe, as the contents were revealed. First there was a lot of packing material, pieces of foam and polythene sheeting quilted with air-bubbles. As this was removed, Don began to pick out some shiny objects from the depths of the crate.

It took only a moment for the Three Detectives to recognize that the shiny objects were weapons and pieces of armor. In fact, as Don removed the items from the crate and Stan stripped them off the wooden display figure, it was clear that the pieces of armor came from identical suits.

There was one difference, though. The pieces that Don removed clanged solidly on the floor as he laid them down; Stan's fell with a softer sound, a sound that was not metallic.

At the same moment all Three Detectives knew that the armor in the crate was made of fiberglass.

Once they had worked this out, they had no problem in guessing what would happen next, and sure enough, Don started to pick up the pieces of armor from the crate and to attach them to the stripped wooden display figure.

They had expected that Stan would then replace the real armor in the crate, but they were surprised to see that instead he reached back into the wooden box, removed more packing, and started to take out the parts of a second suit of armor. So they were going to make two substitutions that night.

The two men worked slowly and methodically. All the time Kevin Parkin continued his restless walking, constantly urging them to hurry up. They kept grumbling that they were doing their best.

Emma felt a gentle breath on her ear and turned to see the outline of Marcus's face very close to hers. "Can you read what it says on the crate?" he breathed softly.

Marcus was very nearsighted, even with his contact lenses in. There was no chance he would be able to read the print on the box at that distance. Emma craned around, careful not to disturb the curtains, but the side of the crate was half-turned away from her and, though she could see there was writing there, the angle was too tight for her to decipher it.

She reached out a hand to tap Stewie's shoulder. He was farther along the edge of the balcony; he would be in a better position to read the writing.

He looked at her. She could see his expression of puzzled inquiry in the half-light. She beckoned him toward her with her little finger.

"What?" Stewie hissed as his head came close to hers.

Gary Bettleton turned sharply and gestured them to silence.

But Emma wanted to know what was printed on the

crate. It could be important in working out the precise nature of Kevin Parkin's crime.

"Can you read the writing on the crate?" she murmured in Stewie's ear.

She looked back to see Gary's expression of annoyance and then heard from below the entertainments manager's voice demand, "What was that?"

They froze, without breathing, as Stan's voice asked, "What was what?"

"I thought I heard something."

"You're imagining things," said Stan.

"I don't know. I'm sure I heard something."

"Probably only the ghost." Don laughed unpleasantly. "Sir Roger Scalethorpe keeping watch for us."

There was a nervous laugh from Kevin Parkin; then he pulled himself together and snapped, "Come on. Get this over with! You're taking forever."

The two men grumbled again and continued with the job at their own pace. Don started putting the second suit of fiberglass armor on the now-bare second dummy, and Stan meticulously packed the two suits of real armor into the crate, wrapping each part in the packing material exactly as the replica pieces had been wrapped.

"Come on, come on," Kevin Parkin urged again, looking angrily at his watch.

"Can't go any faster."

"Nearly there." As he spoke, Stan replaced the lid on the crate and, taking up a hammer that hung from his belt, started to nail it down.

Emma nudged Stewie, who understood what she meant. If the job was nearly over, the men would soon be leaving the armory. They hadn't got much longer to read what was written on the crate.

He edged sideways toward the end of the balcony and moved the curtain a fraction with his hand. Now he had a much clearer view. The three men down below were busy with what they were doing and did not look up. Very slowly, Stewie eased himself forward till he was leaning slightly over the balcony, nearly far enough round to read the printing on the side of the crate. Still, none of the men looked up. He edged a little farther forward.

He would have been fine—except for his pencil flashlight. It was in the top pocket of his dark anorak, and as he craned forward for a better view, the flashlight slipped out. He saw the flash of it falling and reached out a hopeless hand to catch it.

The flashlight fell to the floor of the armory, smashing against the stone with a sound like a thunderclap. Instantly, the three faces below looked up, their expressions a mixture of surprise and fury.

Stewie pulled himself back into the balcony, but not quickly enough. The men did not see him, but they saw the movement of the curtain.

There was a triple roar of anger from below, a hissed "You little idiot!" from Gary Bettleton, then a scramble as the four watchers rushed through the balcony door into the long gallery.

*   *   *

Just as they entered it, bluish light blazed through the gallery's windows, and, only seconds later, the roar of a thunderclap ripped through the sky. The storm, which had been boiling up all day, chose this moment to burst forth, directly above their heads.

The four of them hurtled across the wooden floor. Further flashes of lightning flared, giving even more grotesque shapes to the shadows around them.

Gary reached the door first and grasped the iron ring to open it. But the door seemed stuck. He wrenched at it, twisting the ring ferociously. Emma and Marcus also pulled at the door, trying to help.

It was then that Stewie heard the noise behind them.

Dreading—and somehow knowing—what he would see, he turned slowly around.

At that moment a new flash of blue lightning seared across the long gallery.

Illuminated by it, gliding slowly but inexorably toward him, was the armored figure of Sir Roger Scalethorpe.

15

Outside the Castle

The jammed door gave way at the very moment Stewie saw Sir Roger Scalethorpe approaching. Gary and the other two tumbled through, with Stewie not far behind, and together they all rushed along the maze of murky passages toward the back door. When they'd almost reached it, they heard the angry pounding of Don and Stan's footsteps coming closer, and only just made it out of the castle and into the raging storm.

When they were a safe distance away, they stopped running and looked back, expecting a flood of light and hot pursuit, but there was nothing. Presumably Kevin Parkin and his henchmen didn't want to draw attention to themselves. They didn't want any suspicions going around that something had been happening in the castle that night.

With the danger past, Gary Bettleton became extremely angry. "It was a stupid thing to do in the first place," he raged. "But at least, if we were going to do it, you should have done what I said. All that talking and moving around. I should have known better than to get involved with a bunch of kids!"

"Gary, listen," protested Emma. "It was worth it. Now we've seen what Kevin Parkin's up to. We now know he's a crook."

"We also know he's dangerous. In fact, we knew that before, which is why it was idiotic to go into the castle tonight. Well, we all make mistakes, but rest assured, that's one mistake I'm never going to make again!"

"You mean you're giving up on the case?" asked Marcus.

"You bet I am. I don't care what's going on. I'm going to leave well enough alone."

"But it's not 'well enough.' There's something criminal going on and we've got to stop it."

"There's no 'got to' about it. I don't care what's going on; it has nothing to do with me."

"You mean you won't help us anymore?"

"Yes, that's exactly what I mean! I'm going to forget about the whole thing. And, if you three have any sense, you'll do the same!"

"Oh, Gary, surely you don't mean—"

But Marcus's words came too late. The actor stalked off angrily into the night, leaving the Three Detectives standing drenched and abandoned under the oak tree where they had met a mere hour and a half before.

Marcus looked back at the others. "Well, there goes our most useful ally," he observed glumly.

Emma looked cross. "He's a coward. Just a weak-kneed coward. He doesn't care what's going on, he doesn't care that Lord Scalethorpe's being cheated."

"Now just a minute, we're still not precisely sure what—"

But Emma was too angry to take in Marcus's words. "Never mind, we'll show him. We'll show Gary Bettleton we don't need him. We'll solve the case on our own!"

"Let's hope so." But Marcus didn't sound too confident. Then he looked curiously at the youngest detective. "Are you all right, Stewie?"

"Yes. Sure." But the expression on his face said something different from his words.

"Nothing's happened, has it?" Emma was worried about him, too, now.

"No. No. Just . . ." Stewie paused, then continued, "When we were in the long gallery, when the door jammed, neither of you saw anything, did you?"

"Where?"

"Behind us."

"No. I was trying to get the door open."

Marcus said he had been doing the same. "Why, Stewie, did you see something?"

"Oh . . ."

"What kind of thing did you see?"

"Oh"—Stewie shrugged, as if he didn't care—"nothing."

16

After the Storm

They were all tired when they met the next day after school in Marcus's den. Stewie looked worse than tired. There were dark smudged circles under his eyes and his forehead gleamed uneasily with sweat. He didn't look as if he had slept at all the night before.

But he didn't want to tell the other two what was worrying him. They'd been through all that before. If he started talking about ghosts again, he knew that Marcus would just dismiss the idea.

And yet Stewie had seen what he had seen. He hadn't imagined it. Oh, how he wished one of the others had turned around in the long gallery and seen that frightening figure approaching them. Again, he was the only witness. He was the only one who had seen the knight in armor in the woods. And now he was the only one who had witnessed its second appearance.

Maybe there was something funny in his mind. He felt nervous and twitchy. He only nibbled at the doughnut that Birgit had just brought up to the den, while the other two wolfed theirs hungrily.

When Marcus had finished and had wiped the sugar from around his mouth, he got on to the subject of the night before.

"Well, we're a lot further advanced than we were," he announced.

Emma nodded agreement. "Yes, at least we now know what the crime is."

"We *think* we do. . . ," said Marcus cautiously.

"Oh, come on, it's obvious. Kevin Parkin and his henchmen are replacing the real suits of armor with fiberglass replicas."

"Yes. And then what?"

"Then, presumably, they're selling the originals."

"Fairly difficult to get rid of, I would think, pieces from a collection as famous as that. I mean, the only people in this country who'd be interested in buying armor would be people who know a bit about it, and anyone who knows a bit about it would instantly recognize that these pieces had been stolen from the Scalethorpe collection."

"Well, all right. Then maybe they're selling the stuff abroad." Emma found that Marcus could sometimes be infuriatingly slow. He always wanted all the details of an idea worked out, while she just liked to get the main outline clear.

"Not easy to smuggle something as bulky as that out of the country," Marcus objected. `

"There are ways," said Emma in exasperation. "I mean, okay, we haven't got it all worked out, but the main point is clear. Kevin Parkin is systematically robbing his employer of the Scalethorpe collection of armor."

Marcus still wasn't convinced. "That's the way it looks, I agree, but I wonder if that's all there is to it . . ."

"What more does there need to be to it?" Emma snapped.

"Well, it seems a strange crime, that's all. And it's a crime that can't go undiscovered for long. I mean, you can fool members of the public easily enough with fiberglass replicas, but you can't fool experts. George Kingston said he'd inspected the Scalethorpe collection, and there must be lots of other historians and researchers who'd want to do the same. Okay, the first few times permission's refused, nobody might think too much about it, but eventually people are going to get suspicious. What I'm saying is that the replica suits of armor can only delay the discovery of the theft."

"Yes, but maybe they can delay it long enough . . . buy enough time for Kevin Parkin and his gang to get it all out of the country. Then, before the crime's discovered, they can get away and live very nicely, thank you, on the profits."

"That could be it, yes." Marcus nodded thoughtfully. "I wonder who the rest of the gang were . . ."

"I'm sure Stan and Don were members of the castle staff. Gary definitely recognized them when they appeared."

"Hmm. And no sign of the upper class type with the limp . . ."

"No. Maybe he organizes another part of the operation . . . getting the stuff out of the country perhaps . . ."

"It'd be good if we could ask Gary about Stan and Don."

"We'll be able to in a day or two. Give him a while to calm down. He'll help us again. Last night he was just frightened."

"Hope you're right, Emma." Then Marcus remembered something. "Didn't Gary say he'd get you into the jousting, Stewie?"

"That's right. A week from Saturday."

"Oh well, that's good. You must hold him to that. It'll give us a reason to make contact with him again."

Stewie nodded, but without much enthusiasm. After his shock of the night before, he found it difficult to get enthusiastic about anything.

"Ooh, incidentally, Stewie . . ." Emma suddenly thought of something. "You remember when you leaned out of the balcony . . ."

Stewie shuddered. "Don't remind me of it. I'm hardly likely to forget."

"No, but what I'd forgotten was the reason why you were doing it . . ."

"Oh yes . . ." In all the confusion, Stewie had forgotten that, too.

"Did you read what it said on the side of the crate?"

"Well, yes. Or at least I think I did."

"What do you mean—you *think* you did?" demanded Marcus. "Surely either you did or you didn't."

"I only say that because what was written there just seemed strange."

"What did it say?"

"It said 'Cheeky Charlie Productions.'"

"'Cheeky Charlie Productions!'" the other two echoed in disbelief.

"See what I mean? It does sound odd, doesn't it?"

"You can say that again."

Emma looked thoughtful. "It sounds like something to do with showbiz."

"What do you mean?"

"Well, lots of showbiz companies have strange names. You know, record labels, theatrical managements, that sort of thing."

"Might be worth investigating that area," suggested Marcus, without much hope.

"I'll ask my father," said Emma. "He might have heard the name. And he's got lots of friends in showbiz. He could ask around."

"Worth trying." There was a long silence before Marcus continued. "The question is, what do we do now?"

"Yes . . ."

"I mean, what we've witnessed is pretty well proof that Kevin Parkin is up to something illegal . . ."

"Yes. And just a quick check of the armor could prove it. As soon as someone knows that there are replicas in the armory, Kevin Parkin's got some very awkward questions to answer."

"Right, Emma. But what I'm wondering is, can we do anything more on our own? As the Three Detectives? Or do we have to bring in help?"

"Help?" asked Stewie. "Who do you mean?"

"The police. Should we go and tell the police what we know?"

Emma made a face. "Trouble is, the police might not listen to what they'd regard as 'a bunch of kids.' Also, it would involve us admitting to a bit of trespassing, wouldn't it?"

"That's true. But when they heard what we know—"

"If we were allowed to get as far as telling them what we know. I think it could be risky."

"Well, what else can we do?"

A smile came suddenly to Emma's face. "I've got a much better idea."

"What?"

"I think we should give the information we have to the person who stands to suffer from Kevin Parkin's little games."

"You mean we should go to—"

"Yes. I think we should tell Lord Scalethorpe."

✤ 17 ✤

Lord Scalethorpe

When Lord Scalethorpe's photograph had appeared in the previous Monday's *Daily Telegraph,* the accompanying report had said that he was going to be in America for a week. So, after school on the next Monday Emma, reckoning he must be back, rang the castle and asked to speak to him. The Three Detectives had agreed that she should be the one to make contact; the boys considered that she was better than they were at that sort of thing.

The castle switchboard put her through to Lord Scalethorpe's secretary, Mrs. Wilson. "I'm afraid he's not in the office today," a guarded female voice answered.

"Well, I wondered if I could make an appointment to see him the next time he is in."

"May I ask who's speaking?" asked the voice cautiously.

"My name's Emma Cobbett."

"And in what connection was it that you wished to see his Lordship?"

This was a difficult question to answer. Emma didn't want to give too much away to a complete stranger. Who could say which members of the castle staff were part of Kevin Parkin's conspiracy?

"It's something very important. Something to do with the castle."

"Yes. . . ?"

The voice didn't sound convinced of its importance. Emma was going to have to give away a little more to secure her interview.

"Someone is trying to cheat Lord Scalethorpe. He doesn't know what's happening, and I want to tell him, so that he can put a stop to it."

"I see." The voice still wasn't convinced. Emma wished she sounded more grown-up on the phone; people didn't take a voice like hers seriously.

"Well, look, Miss Cobbett, I will pass on your message to Lord Scalethorpe. But you must understand, he's a very busy man. It may not be possible for him to spare the time to see you."

"It is important, I promise."

"Yes, well, I will tell him that. Give me your phone number and I'll get back to you one way or the other."

When Emma put the phone down, she didn't feel very confident that the secretary would get back to her. The voice had been dismissive and patronizing; the secretary didn't sound as if she was going to press Emma's cause very hard.

Still, there was nothing else she could do for the time being. She'd give it a couple of days, then try to make contact with Lord Scalethorpe again. And, if that failed, the Three Detectives would have to think of some other approach to the case.

It was frustrating. They knew so much, and yet they didn't know enough. Everything seemed rather flat after the excitement of Thursday night. Emma felt at loose ends. There must be something else she could do in the investigation . . .

Hmm. When her father came home, of course, she could ask him whether he had ever heard of Cheeky Charlie Productions. There might be some sort of lead there . . .

Meanwhile, boring old ordinary life had to go on. Emma settled down to do her French homework.

When Douglas Cobbett got back from work, his daughter asked him about Cheeky Charlie Productions. He shook his head. Never heard of them. Yes, okay, he'd make some inquiries. He was in the middle of directing an episode of a police series. He'd ask around the cast.

Emma went back to her French homework. Everything still felt very flat and boring.

But things perked up the next day. When she got back from school, her stepmother gave her a message. A Mrs. Wilson had called. Could Emma call her back?

Emma called immediately.

"Oh, good afternoon, Miss Cobbett. I mentioned your call to Lord Scalethorpe and he said, yes, he would like to arrange a meeting with you." The secretary could not keep out of her voice her surprise at how he had reacted. "Now, his Lordship would be available Thursday afternoon or Friday morning. I wonder if either of those times might be convenient. . . ?"

Emma arranged to come to his office at four-thirty on Thursday afternoon. She felt gleeful as she put the phone down. The lull was over. Things were starting to happen again. She picked up the phone excitedly to tell Marcus and Stewie the good news.

The office into which Emma was ushered by Lord Scalethorpe's secretary was in a part of the castle that the public did not visit. It was not near the empty, untended rooms through which Gary and the Three Detectives had passed the previous week, but in a tower whose doors were marked PRIVATE. ESTATE OFFICES.

The office itself had panelled walls and reassuringly old and expensive-looking furniture. Glass-fronted bookcases housed leather-bound books. Before the large fireplace a brass fender winked in the afternoon light, which streamed through the diamond panes of the windows.

And the man who stood up to greet Emma was also reassuringly old and expensive-looking. She recognized him from his photograph in the newspaper, but in the flesh he was more impressive. He was taller than she expected; the gray hair was more distinguished, the black eyebrows bushier.

He reached a hand across the desk and shook hers firmly. "Good afternoon," he said in a deep, cultured voice, and indicated a high, leather-upholstered armchair for her to sit in.

"Thank you, Mrs. Wilson." As he sat down, he gestured to his secretary, who left the room, looking rather disgruntled that she was not to be included in the conference.

"Now, Miss Cobbett," said Lord Scalethorpe, "what can I do for you? Mrs. Wilson said you had something important to tell me."

"Yes, I have." Emma took a deep breath, and then launched in. "You are being robbed, Lord Scalethorpe."

"What!" the bushy eyebrows shot up, but there was still a slight humor in his expression, an infuriating look of patronage. He grinned. "Well, I know I'm being robbed by the taxman, but who else do you reckon is after my belongings?"

It was a straight question, and Emma gave it a straight answer. "Your entertainments manager, Kevin Parkin."

"What!" The eyebrows shot up again, but this time there was no hint of humor in Lord Scalethorpe's face. The shock had been completely genuine. "What on earth do you mean?"

"Kevin Parkin, with some assistance from other members of the castle staff, is systematically stealing the Scalethorpe collection of armor."

His face turned very pale; he looked instantly older. "How are they doing it?" he asked softly.

"They're replacing the genuine armor with fiberglass replicas."

"And what are they doing with the real armor?"

"I don't know. Presumably getting it out of the castle and selling it off somewhere. Probably abroad."

"You don't know how?"

"No."

The owner of Scalethorpe Castle was silent. He looked deeply agitated. His hands fiddled nervously with a paper-knife on his desk. Emma said nothing.

Eventually he spoke. "What you say is most peculiar."

"It's true. It really is."

"Yes, I'm inclined to believe you. If only because it's too strange an idea for anyone to make up." He suddenly flashed a shrewd look at her from under his bushy eyebrows. "Of course, what you tell me does raise one interesting question."

"What's that?"

"How you have found out about what you claim is going on."

She had known that this question must come up in time, and she knew that there was going to be no escape from the truth. She would have to admit the Three Detectives' trespass into the castle.

"I saw Kevin and his men substituting two suits of armor last Thursday night."

"You mean you were inside the castle?" he asked, amazed.

"Yes."

"But how on earth did you get in?"

"Someone helped. He had a key to the back door."

"Who was that someone?"

Emma hesitated. She didn't want to get Gary into trouble.

But Lord Scalethorpe quickly reassured her. "Don't worry. I'm not going to take any action against you for illegal entry. If what you say is true, I'll be so grateful to you for bringing the crime to my attention that I won't care what methods you used to find out about it."

"Oh, it's true, sure enough. All you have to do is tap your knuckles against some of the suits of armor in the armory, and you'll find out they're fiberglass."

"Good," said Lord Scalethorpe. "So who was it who let you into the castle?"

There could be no harm in telling. Indeed, Gary might benefit from his employer's generosity for helping to uncover the crime. "Gary Bettleton."

"Ah. My Merry Andrew."

"Yes."

Lord Scalethorpe nodded and was silent again for a moment. He still looked troubled, but as if he was coming to terms with the shock and was now planning what he should do about it.

Finally he spoke. "Miss Cobbett, I can't thank you enough for coming to see me. It was a very sensible thing to do, and I am more grateful than I can say for the information you have given me. Obviously, I'll have to check the details, but I'm sure that in outline it's right. As a matter of fact, it would tie in well with certain suspicions that I've held for some time about my entertainments manager. Yes . . ." He paused, thoughtful. "Yes, it does make sense of quite a lot of things. Hmm."

He gave her another piercing look. "I must ask you, however, please to keep quiet about your suspicions to anyone else for the time being. At the appropriate moment, of course, when everything has been checked, the police will be brought in. But I don't want the thieves warned that I'm on to them before that. So, please, absolute secrecy for the time being."

"You can rely on all of us."

"All of us? So it wasn't just you and Gary Bettleton who broke into the castle?"

"No, there were two others. Friends of mine."

"Oh, please give me their names. When everything's sorted out, I would like to see that you are all rewarded for what you have done."

"Don't worry. We didn't do it because we hoped to get anything out of it."

"Well, if not rewarded, at least thanked. What are your friends' names?"

Emma gave the names of the other two detectives, and Lord Scalethorpe wrote them down on a note pad. Then he looked at his watch.

"Miss Cobbett, I'm sorry, we must leave it there. I

have a great deal to do—particularly after what you've told me. Don't worry, the culprits will be brought to justice. I will see to it that you are informed once everything is sorted out. And"—he rose again from his seat and reached across the desk to shake her hand—"I can't thank you enough for what you have done. You and your friends may well have saved Scalethorpe Castle!"

✤ 18 ✤

The Squire

It was of course very satisfactory that the case was now out of their hands, but none of the Three Detectives could deny that it left them feeling rather flat. They had done the right thing in giving all the information to Lord Scalethorpe, and no doubt in time they would hear of the successful outcome of the case, when Kevin Parkin and his henchmen were arrested. But they felt slightly cheated by not being in at the climax of the case themselves. It was like reading a whodunit, only to find that the last chapter was missing.

Still, there was not a lot they could do about it. They would just have to get on with their normal lives until another case came up. So Emma decided to step up her tennis coaching, and Marcus started to devise a computer program against which he could play Trivial Pursuit.

Stewie, on the other hand, couldn't settle down to anything. He tried to get back to the invention he had been working on before he first saw the knight in armor—a device that would peel and slice cucumbers and then put them into sandwiches—but he couldn't concentrate. And he knew he wouldn't be able to concentrate until he had found a logical explanation for the two appearances of the figure who looked like Sir Roger Scalethorpe.

He still hadn't told the others what he had seen in the long gallery, and the first panicky fear had soon subsided. But he was left with an unsatisfied sensation. Logic told him that ghosts didn't exist. Therefore what he had seen could not have been a ghost. All the same, he had definitely seen it, and he wanted an explanation.

That was one of the reasons why he called Gary Bettleton on Thursday evening. He didn't want to ask Gary directly about the apparition in the long gallery, but he thought he might be able to work around to the subject. The other reason for his call was to see if Gary really could get him in to watch the jousting at Scalethorpe Castle the following Saturday.

The actor sounded guarded and suspicious when he heard who was on the other end of the phone. "I told you," he said, "I'm not going to have anything more to do with the case. I just don't want to know about it."

"It's all right," Stewie assured him. "We've all come to the same conclusion."

"You have?"

"Yes. There was nothing more we could do, so we've given it up." Stewie didn't say that they'd only given it up because they'd passed it over to Lord Scalethorpe. That might well get Gary all suspicious again.

"You really mean that?"

"Yes. So far as we're concerned, the case is over."

"Well, I'm very glad to hear it." Gary's voice was instantly more relaxed. "There are some things one just shouldn't meddle with."

Stewie took advantage of the actor's change of mood to say, "Anyway, that wasn't what I was calling about. I wanted to talk about the jousting."

"Jousting?"

"Yes, you said you were going to be jousting on Saturday."

"That's right."

"And you said that you'd somehow get me in to watch."

"Good heavens, yes. So I did."

"What I'm calling to ask is: Is that offer still on?"

"Well, yes, I suppose it is . . ." Suddenly Gary Bettleton seemed to have an idea. "Just a minute. Yes, actually this could be very good."

"What?"

"The way the jousting's set up, we're all supposed to be knights, and we have squires who pass us the weapons and things. Well, I just heard at the castle today that the lad who usually acts as my squire has the flu. There's no chance he's going to be fit by Saturday."

105

Stewie could hardly believe his ears. "So what are you suggesting?"

"I'm suggesting that you stand in for him. How'd you like to act as my squire in the tournament?"

"You bet!" said Stewie.

On Saturday morning the tilting yard of Scalethorpe Castle was being prepared for the afternoon's entertainment. It was a colorful scene. Along the middle a barrier had been set up and hung with brightly colored banners. It was on either side of this that the knights would gallop up on their horses to do battle. Multicolored flags were also fixed to the barriers behind which the members of the public would gather to watch the day's excitements.

Dominating the tilting yard was a platform, also hung with bright draperies, where a throne and other gilded chairs commanded the best view of the proceedings. Everything about it looked medieval, except for the pair of microphones fixed in front of the throne.

"That," Gary Bettleton explained to his new squire, "is where the king sits."

"King?"

"Yes, the whole show's set up as if it's all being laid on as entertainment for the king."

"Who is the king, though?"

"He's that fat oaf who acts as Lord of the Revels in the medieval banquets."

"Oh yes, I saw him on *OOPS!*"

Gary winced. "Ugh. You know, rumor has it that they're coming back here to do another program."

"Last one of the series, I think. Their Awards Special. A live broadcast."

The actor shuddered at the thought. Perhaps it was the memory of being pilloried and pelted with rotten fruit and eggs that made him uncomfortable.

"Anyway, Stewie, let me show you where everything is. You see, basically, once the show starts, I'm up on horseback and can't reach down for the various weapons I need, so you have to hand them to me. Look, they're all over here."

He indicated a rack in which were propped a series of lances, a large warsword, a battleaxe, and a knobbly mace.

"Those look fairly terrifying."

Gary Bettleton grinned. "Yes, but don't worry. We've rehearsed every move of this a thousand times, and the horses are brilliantly trained. There's no danger of anyone getting hurt. All that matters is that you hand me the right weapon at the right time."

"How will I know which *is* the right one?"

"It's quite easy." Gary pointed to a small blackboard leaning against the weapon rack. "The running order of the fights is written down there. Look, you see it says, SINGLE JOUST, AXE-FIGHT, QUINTAIN, and so on. You do know what a quintain is, by the way, don't you?"

"Oh, yes. It's one of those pivoted targets that swings around and thumps you one if you don't hit it right."

"Exactly. There it is."

Gary pointed to a strange object that projected above one end of the central barrier. It was shaped like the torso of a man. Both arms stuck out. From one a series of rings hung down, from the other a heavy metal ball on a chain.

"You see, what we have to do for the quintain routine is gallop up and try to get the rings on the end of our lances. If you get them cleanly, they just come off and the quintain hardly moves. If you hit the arm, though . . ."

"The metal ball comes around and thumps you."

"Exactly. Can be quite painful, actually. Oh, one thing, Stewie, we use different lances for the quintain and the actual jousting. For the quintain we use this one." He indicated a lance with a long sharp point. "You need that if you're going to hook off the rings. When we're actually jousting, we use these." He pointed to a row of lances with slightly thicker ends. "Not only are we less likely to do each other any damage with these blunt ones, they're also made so that the last part's detachable." He twisted off a six-foot section from one of them to demonstrate his point. "These ends are very fragile, likely to break on impact. That looks good from the point of view of the audience, and, of course, it's another safety precaution. You can't do anyone much harm with one of these."

Stewie looked at the two sorts of lances as Gary replaced them.

"The important thing is," the actor continued, "that you give me the right one at the right time. It's easy to tell them apart. Remember, slightly thicker ends are for jousting, and the pointed ends are just for the quintain. Got that?"

"Yes."

"Whatever you do, don't get that wrong. If I gallop up to my opponent and hit him with one of the sharp lances, I'm not going to do him a lot of good."

"No. Don't worry. I've got it."

"Right. Look, I'll explain where you stand and so on as we go along. Better just go and find you a costume that's going to fit."

"Do I get to dress up?"

"Of course you do. Come on."

The actor led his new squire into a small outbuilding on the edge of the tilting yard. Inside were rows of pegs, on which were hanging coats of chain-mail, surcoats, shields, and banners.

There was also a weasel-faced boy of about Stewie's age, who looked up sharply as they entered.

"Oh, hello, Keith," said Gary.

The boy looked at Stewie with an expression that was a mixture of surprise and hostility. "Who's this?"

"My new squire for this afternoon."

"Stewart Hinde," said Stewie, holding out his hand.

"Oh." The boy gave him a piercing look, then turned abruptly, and walked out of the building.

"Who's he?"

Gary looked up from the pile of costumes he was riffling through. "Oh, that's your opposite number. He's the squire to Sir Jasper Greville, the Black Knight."

"The Black Knight, eh? That sounds evil."

"Yes, the whole show's set up with goodies and baddies. I'm Sir Percival, the Red Knight. Real goody-goody. Flower of chivalry, all that rubbish."

"It sounds as if it's great fun."

"I suppose it is, the first time," said Gary wearily. "Trouble is, when you've been doing it every two weeks for a couple of years, the novelty wears off. Here, try these things for size."

Stewie was handed a chain mail coat, a pair of chain mail leggings, and a brightly colored tunic to wear over them. He was surprised at how light it all felt.

"This is not real chain mail."

"Good heavens, no. It's just painted knitting . . . the sort of stuff that's been used in theaters for years. It'd be impossible to do the show in the real stuff. So hot, for a start. And it'd weigh you down horribly."

"But do you wear steel breastplates and things?"

"No, just this."

"So you've got no protection if you get hit?"

"We don't get hit. We take all the blows on the shield, you see. As I said, the whole routine's rehearsed down to the last detail. All the falls are rehearsed, everything."

"Oh." Stewie sounded almost disappointed.

"Come on, try it on," said Gary.

Stewie slipped on the squire's armor over his normal clothes. "How's it look?"

"Terrific, squire," said Gary Bettleton.

✣ 19 ✣

The Tournament

Marcus and Emma wouldn't have missed the tournament for anything. For a start, they wanted to be there to see Stewie's performance as the squire. And the idea of the jousting itself was intriguing; they wanted to see how the Middle Ages could be brought to life in the twentieth century.

Besides, Scalethorpe Castle still exercised a magnetic attraction on them. Although the case was now out of their hands, they remained deeply interested in the strange goings-on they had witnessed and felt that somehow, by being on the spot, they might find out more about the mystery.

The proceedings were due to start at two-thirty. It was a sunny afternoon and a large crowd had gathered at the gate to the tilting yard. From their conversations it was

111

clear that many of them had come because of the *OOPS!* program, once again proving the publicity power of television.

But Emma and Marcus found it easy to forget the twentieth century when they were actually in their seats. The blazing colors of the banners and drapery looked magnificent in the sunlight, and it was possible to believe that this was how the tilting yard had looked some five hundred years before, when knights had assembled for real tournaments.

The historical atmosphere was quickly broken, however, when the afternoon's proceedings began. The fat man who had been Master of the Revels in the banqueting hall, now looking very hot in a purple velvet gown and heavy crown, mounted the platform and, as he did so, knocked against his throne, which wobbled dangerously.

He immediately turned to the microphones and said, "OOPS!"

The audience gave a delighted laugh of recognition. Emma looked at Marcus ruefully. They weren't going to be in for an afternoon of medieval magic; it looked as if it would be just more cheap television slapstick.

The "king" was joined on the platform by a couple of apologetic-looking girls in long gowns and hats like upturned ice-cream cones. Then two page-boy figures in colorful tabards appeared, carrying long trumpets.

A crackly fanfare began to be heard over the loudspeakers in the yard. Seconds too late, the page-boys raised their trumpets to their lips and mimed blowing. The fanfare stopped abruptly and, again seconds too late, the boys stopped miming and lowered their trumpets.

The king came forward to the microphone and raised his hands for silence. "My lords, ladies, peasants, serfs, vassals, and other medieval riff-raff, welcome to Scalethorpe Castle and my tournament. I, as those of ye who have watched *OOPS!* on ye goggle-box may know, am ye king. So what I say, goes. Got that? Okay."

Emma looked at Marcus again and they both winced. It seemed sad that such a lovely setting should be ruined by this kind of broad, nudging performance.

Still, the afternoon perked up when the king finally came to the end of his string of weak jokes and introduced "the doughty knights who are to do battle for their ladies' honors here this afternoon."

They were introduced one by one and looked truly magnificent as they galloped in, high on their huge horses. Each knight's head was hidden in a tall jousting helm, shaped a bit like an upturned coal-scuttle. Over their knitted chain-mail they wore coats in their distinctive colors and these were matched by draperies on the horses. There was a Blue Knight, a Yellow Knight, Sir Percival the Red Knight, and, bigger and more fearsome-looking than the rest, Sir Jasper the Black Knight.

"Oh, look, there's Stewie!" Emma pointed to the small armored figure who was standing by the rack of weapons at the far end of the tilting yard.

"This is his idea of heaven," said Marcus, "actually being part of history. It's what he's always dreamed of."

"And now," the voice of the king, distorted through the loudspeakers, boomed, "let ye tournament begin!"

Once the actual jousting started, it was very impressive. The four knights were in two teams—the Blue Knight supporting Sir Percival, and the Yellow Knight Sir Jasper. They started by fighting one against one, first the Blue Knight and the Yellow Knight thundering toward each other with lances at the ready, hitting fiercely against each other's shields and smashing both lance-tips in the encounter. It was very exciting; the ground beneath them shook and the sound of the pounding hooves echoed off the stone walls of the castle.

Then it was the turn of Sir Jasper and Sir Percival to joust. The audience were encouraged to support their favorites, and Emma and Marcus, knowing whose face was under the Red Knight's helmet, shouted loudly for Gary.

This time the two knights came together with such an impact that both were unseated from their saddles. They picked themselves up, threw aside their shields and splintered lances, and turned to their squires, who were running toward them with heavy warswords, each weapon nearly as tall as a man.

Stewie handed the Red Knight his sword, and the weasel-faced boy gave the Black Knight his. Then the two armored figures went into the attack.

Emma and Marcus knew the fight must have been

carefully rehearsed, but it still looked dangerous. The swords were so heavy that even a glancing blow would have been pretty painful, but the two fighters managed to parry accurately and miss each other by inches. It was a good demonstration of split-second timing, and when the king finally ordered the knights to be separated, they got an enthusiastic round of applause from the audience.

The next contest was to be the quintain. The King, with more feeble jokes, explained how the device worked and what the knights were aiming for, and announced that the honors would be contested once again between Sir Percival and Sir Jasper. (Marcus got the impression that the Blue and Yellow Knights were still learning the business and weren't allowed to do any of the more elaborate routines.)

Sir Jasper was to go first, and he took off his helmet to shout defiant insults at his opponent.

"Marcus!"

He heard Emma hiss his name and followed her pointing finger to the face that was now revealed.

It was a face they recognized, a face that they had last seen at midnight in the Scalethorpe Castle armory.

"Don!" Marcus murmured.

But that was not the only surprise in store for them that afternoon. Sir Jasper began his attacks on the quintain, carrying off one of the rings at his first attempt. He raised his lance in triumph, and jeered more insults at Sir Percival.

115

"It's strange," Marcus whispered to Emma. "I'd have thought Lord Scalethorpe would have got the police on to them by now."

"Well, clearly he hasn't. Look!"

This time Emma's finger pointed only a few rows in front of them. Just taking up his seat was the unmistakable short figure of the castle's entertainments manager, Kevin Parkin.

The quintain competition continued. Each knight removed two rings, then Sir Jasper failed to secure a third, and Sir Percival started his gallop to get the last ring and win the contest.

But, unseen by him, on the other side of the barrier, Sir Jasper's weasel-faced squire had crept up and, just as the galloping knight approached, swung the quintain around to destroy his aim. As Sir Percival passed, the swinging ball came around and caught him a resounding blow on the back.

He reined his horse and turned angrily to the Royal Box.

"My liege," shouted Sir Percival, giving a good demonstration of Gary Bettleton's acting training, "Sir Jasper is a cheat! I demand that he shall fight me in single combat that I may avenge his insult!"

This, too, had obviously been rehearsed, but it was still very dramatic.

And even more dramatic when Sir Jasper suddenly galloped forward to demand that Sir Percival withdraw

116

his words. Don wasn't nearly such a good actor as Gary, but he looked threateningly large on his huge horse.

"Never!" cried Sir Percival. Then, removing the gauntlet from his right hand, he flung it into his opponent's face. "There, Sir Jasper! I challenge you!"

Sir Jasper just managed to catch the glove before it fell. "And I accept the challenge!"

"Then," cried the fat king, "let battle commence!"

As the two knights galloped back toward their squires, Marcus suddenly froze. He had heard a voice that he recognized. "Sorry I'm late," it said. "Got held up."

There was no question. It was the upper class voice he had heard talking to Kevin Parkin in the armory. It was the entertainments manager's partner-in-crime.

He looked toward the source of the sound, and saw a tall, gray-haired figure limping along the row ahead toward Kevin Parkin.

Marcus seized Emma's arm and hissed, "Look, down there. It's the man I heard in the armory!"

"Is it? Are you sure?"

"Yes, of course I'm sure. I'd recognize that voice anywhere." He felt her body go rigid. "Why, Emma, what's the matter?"

"That man," she murmured, "is Lord Scalethorpe!"

Stewie took the pointed lance from Sir Percival and handed up one with a breakable end.

"Well done," said Gary.

117

"At least thank goodness I got that right. Don't want you skewering your opponent, do we?"

"No," said the actor. "Be ready to bring the mace when I fall off."

"You know you're going to fall off?"

"All rehearsed to the last detail, Stewie." Gary Bettleton grinned, then replaced his helmet. Giving his horse a reassuring pat, he tucked the lance into the crook of his right arm, raised the shield on his left, and, with a twitch at the reins, started to gallop toward the barrier.

At the same moment Stewie looked at the other end of the tilting yard. Sir Jasper had also turned his horse for the attack. But the weasel-faced squire had done nothing. There had been no exchange of weapons.

Under Sir Jasper's arm was still fixed a lance with a deadly sharp end.

Stewie rushed forward, shouting a warning.

But it was too late. The jousting knights came together with a tremendous crunch, and mixed in with the sound was a shriek of human pain. Sir Percival was unseated and fell back to the ground with a heavy thud that dislodged his helmet.

By the time Stewie reached him, Gary Bettleton's eyes were closed. His face was unnaturally pale. And pinning his wooden shield to his chest was the splintered shaft of Sir Jasper's lance.

Blood had already seeped through the knitted chainmail and was spreading across the grass.

✤ 20 ✤

Hospital

Marcus's face was set in an expression of unusual seriousness. "It changes quite a lot of things, doesn't it?" he said.

The other two detectives nodded. They were back in Marcus's den. Birgit had produced a tray of Cokes and buns, but the food lay untouched. They were too shocked to do more than sip at their drinks.

"It must mean that Lord Scalethorpe's involved in the crime, mustn't it?"

Marcus nodded. "There can't be any other explanation, Emma."

"Oh, the hypocrisy of it!" she burst out. "All that business about saving British art treasures from going abroad, and all the time he's actually sending off his own precious suits of armor."

119

Marcus was cautious, as ever. "We're not sure that that's what's going on. We still haven't worked out the precise details and can't be positive that—"

"No," Emma interrupted, "but we can be positive that Lord Scalethorpe is in it right up to his neck!"

"Yes, there's no question about that. From what I overheard him say in the armory, he knew all about it. But because he and Kevin Parkin were joking about 'Lord Scalethorpe' in the third person, it never occurred to me that the other man might be Lord Scalethorpe himself."

"And, in fact, by telling him our suspicions, we just gave him warning that someone was on to them. We played right into their hands." Emma looked extremely glum.

"Yes." Marcus sighed. "Oh, if only I'd been the one to go and see him. I'd have recognized the voice instantly."

"Or if he'd done more than just get up from his desk when I went to see him, I might have noticed his limp and got suspicious."

"Mind you, it does explain why he was so ready to see you after your phone call."

"Oh dear. We really have messed things up, haven't we?"

"Especially for Gary," said Stewie softly. He had been quiet for an unusually long time. The shock of the afternoon's events had hit him harder than it had the others.

"Yes, poor Gary."

"And that was our fault, Emma."

"What on earth do you mean?"

"Look . . ." Stewie spoke quickly and passionately. "If you hadn't given Lord Scalethorpe Gary's name—and I'm not blaming you, any one of us would have done exactly the same thing—but if we'd kept his name out of it, he wouldn't have been injured this afternoon."

Emma went pale. "You're right. I was still sort of trying to pretend to myself that what happened today in the tilting yard was an accident."

Stewie shook his blond head firmly. "No. That was no accident. Oh, it looked like an accident. The audience thought it was an accident. And I've no doubt, when the police come to investigate it, they'll get some story about the squire not concentrating or Don getting carried away in the emotion of the moment and forgetting to change the lance. They wouldn't know that anyone had any motive against Gary, so they may well end up thinking it was an accident, too. But it wasn't. Look, I was just doing my first afternoon as squire, but even I knew which lances to use for which parts of the tournament. The other squire's been doing it for ages. He wouldn't make a mistake unless someone had given him strict instructions to do so."

"So you think he's part of the gang, too?"

"It looks that way. No, what happened to Gary this

afternoon was carefully planned, a deliberate, cold-blooded attempt to warn us all off."

"What do you mean?"

"Because Gary's older than us, the gang must've reckoned he was the ringleader in our investigations. So they've put him out of action—in a particularly nasty way."

"Oh, I wonder how he is," said Emma anxiously.

"He was still unconscious when the ambulance took him away."

"Yes. He'd lost a lot of blood."

"Let's just hope and pray that he pulls through," said Marcus.

"What, you think he might not?"

"It was a very serious injury. If the lance went near his heart . . . Remember what happened to Sir Roger Scalethorpe."

"Oh, no!"

"Then we'd be up against not just a gang of crooks, but a gang of murderers." Marcus was silent while he let this idea sink in.

"We must call the hospital and find out how Gary is," said Emma.

"Yes," Marcus agreed grimly. "Anyway, it certainly confirms what they said about not being afraid to use violence."

"Right. And they no doubt hope that what happened to Gary will frighten us, too, and make us keep our mouths shut."

"We can't be sure that that's what they intended."

"Yes, we can, Emma," Stewie said firmly. "They left me in no doubt about it."

"They talked to you?"

"After Gary had been taken off in the ambulance, I went to that small building on the edge of the tilting yard to take off my costume. Don was in there."

"Was he shocked by what had happened?"

"No. If anything, it seemed to amuse him. But he said to me, in a sort of unpleasant, half-joking way, 'Poor old Gary. Nasty accident, wasn't it?' And then he said, 'Still, just goes to show what happens to people who poke their noses in where they don't belong. Doesn't it?'"

"Hmm."

"Now you're not going to tell me that wasn't a warning, are you?"

Marcus was all caution again. "It certainly does sound peculiar, but we can't be certain that—"

"Oh, don't be ridiculous!" Emma snapped. "That was an absolutely clear warning. They were telling us that they knew what we knew, and that if we didn't stop investigating the case, we too might be in danger of having some kind of 'accident.'"

There was a silence. Then Stewie voiced the question that was in all their minds. "So are we going to stop investigating the case?"

As one, the Three Detectives shook their heads.

* * *

123

When they called on Sunday morning, the news from the hospital could have been worse. Gary Bettleton had lost a great deal of blood and was very feeble, but he had regained consciousness. His wound had been dressed and he was no longer on the danger list. And yes, it would be possible for him to have visitors, so long as they didn't stay too long.

The Three Detectives went to see him on Sunday evening. The nurse on the ward said she could only allow them in one at a time, and they were only allowed to stay for five minutes each. "He's still very weak," she said. "Needs a lot of rest."

Emma went first. Gary was in a private room, looking horribly pale and feeble, heavily bandaged and propped up on pillows. He did not seem particularly pleased to see her.

She had brought him a box of chocolates, which she put on the bedside table. He thanked her.

She asked how he was. He said he was bearing up.

She said she was terribly sorry about his injury. How on earth could something like that happen?

When she asked this, a gleam of fear came into Gary's eyes.

"It was an accident," he said in a fierce whisper. "Understand that—it was an accident! And if anyone says otherwise, it's been made pretty clear that I could be the victim of another accident. But a second time I might not get off so lightly!"

*   *   *

124

Emma's five minutes were soon up. Marcus went in next. Then he came and sat with Emma in the waiting room, while Stewie went in to see the invalid.

When the third detective returned, he looked as glum as the other two. He sat down disconsolately. "I'm afraid it's worked. Lord Scalethorpe and his gang wanted to frighten Gary off, and they've succeeded. He knows exactly what happened, but he's far too scared ever to breathe a word about it."

Marcus nodded. "Yes, and he virtually told us to keep our mouths shut, too."

"It puts us in a difficult position, doesn't it?" said Emma. "I mean, if we go on investigating, we may be putting Gary in even more danger. He's absolutely helpless in the hospital, and I wouldn't put it past this gang to come here and do him further injury."

"That seems to be what he's afraid of," said Stewie. "I got the impression he's been threatened somehow since he's been here in the hospital."

Marcus made a rueful face. "They've really got us, haven't they? Their little plan seems to have worked. Gary's been frightened off, and, and, because of the threat to him, we can't do anything either."

They subsided into a gloomy silence.

Then Emma suddenly pointed to someone walking along the corridor toward Gary's room. "Look! I recognize that man."

Stewie leaped to his feet. "It's not one of the Scalethorpe gang, is it?"

"No. I recognize him from the television. It's Michael Bettleton."

"Gary's brother? The reporter?"

"That's right."

"Good. Let's wait here till he comes out."

"Yes," said Emma. "I've got a feeling that Michael Bettleton may be just the person we need to help us!"

✤ 21 ✤

The Reporter

Gary Bettleton's brother was not allowed to stay with the invalid much longer than the Three Detectives had been, and it was only ten minutes later that they saw him walking back along the corridor toward them.

Emma rose to her feet and intercepted him. "Excuse me. You're Michael Bettleton, aren't you?"

His face, which had been troubled and preoccupied, at once took on the professional smile of a public figure greeting a fan. "Yes, that's right. How flattering to be recognized. I didn't realize my program was popular with the younger audience."

"Well, I watch it sometimes," said Emma, unwilling to give him too much grounds for self-congratulation. "We want to talk to you about your brother."

The other two detectives had joined her now as Michael Bettleton said, "My brother? Gary? You mean you know him?"

"Yes."

"Well, as you've no doubt heard, he's had rather a serious accident."

"Yes, we know."

"Except," said Stewie, "that it wasn't an accident."

They explained further in the hospital's coffee shop. In spite of the danger to Gary, they told Michael Bettleton everything. After all, as a brother, he had a right to know the full story. Also, as an investigative reporter, he might be able to help them solve the case.

It was clear when they had finished that he was both very interested and very angry. "To think what they did to Gary! They could have killed him!"

"Yes," Marcus agreed. "And they might yet, if they find out we're still trying to get them."

Michael looked thoughtful. "There must be some way we can catch them. Of course I'd have to double-check all the facts. You're certain about the substitution of the armor?"

"Yes, there's no question about that."

"And you reckon they're shipping the stuff abroad and selling it?"

"We think they must be. Apparently no one would touch it in this country. It's all too famous."

"Yes, but abroad they might not be so fussy, might not ask too many questions about where it had come from.

Hmm, yes, that sounds possible. What did you say was written on the crate?"

"Cheeky Charlie Productions."

"Well, I can try and check that out."

"My father's making some inquiries. I thought it sounded a bit like a showbiz name."

"Good thinking, Emma. In fact, you've all done very well to get this far. The question is: What do we do next?"

Michael Bettleton's mind was moving quickly. Immediately he was thinking like a professional reporter, and it was flattering to the Three Detectives that he was treating them as equals in his plans of investigation.

"There are one or two obvious things we can do," he continued. "It might not be a bad idea if I were to pose as a historical researcher and ask if I could examine the armor. Be interesting to see what reaction I get . . ."

"Don't you think your name would make them suspicious?"

He grinned. "I'm sure it would—if I used it. No, I'm afraid in my line of business you get rather used to using false names and what-have-you. That wouldn't be a problem." Another thought came to him. "Hmm. I wonder how much Gary'll be prepared to tell me. . . ?"

"Very little, I bet," said Marcus. "He's so frightened."

"Yes." Once again Michael Bettleton was angry. "Oh, I'd really like to get them for what they've done to my brother. He's sometimes a bit weak and indecisive, but he's never intended anyone any harm in his life. Don't worry, we'll nail them somehow."

"But we've got to get all of them," Emma insisted, "particularly Lord Scalethorpe. The others are just vicious thugs, but he's the really evil one. He's been completely two-faced about the whole business."

"Yes, and I bet his little plan was to get off scot-free."

"What do you mean?"

"Well, I'm only guessing, but I wouldn't be surprised if he planned to turn the rest of the gang over to the police, anyway."

"How? Sorry, I don't understand."

Michael Bettleton pieced his thoughts together slowly. "Look, as you've said, the crime can't go on undiscovered for long, so Lord Scalethorpe must be planning for the moment when it is found out. Let's just imagine that the planning goes like this: The real armor is replaced by the fiberglass stuff and somehow shipped out of the country, where it's sold. Some of the profit on the sale goes to Kevin Parkin and his gang, and some of it comes back to Lord Scalethorpe . . . in a way that can't be traced.

"Then, maybe, at a prearranged time, Parkin and his gang disappear . . . go abroad to live on their proceeds of the robbery. At that point Lord Scalethorpe allows someone to inspect the armor. It's all found to be forgeries, there's a great fuss in the press, Lord Scalethorpe says he's heartbroken, he's lost all his heritage, and so on and so on. He gets lots of public sympathy, everyone feels very sorry for him. And then he claims the value of what's been stolen on his insurance."

"So he gets money for the armor twice?"

"That's right, Marcus. I bet he's got some clever way of hiding the fact that he's profiting from the sale of the stuff. From the sound of Kevin Parkin, he's not very bright. Someone like Lord Scalethorpe could run circles around him."

"So Parkin and his pals would be cheated, too?"

"It wouldn't surprise me. Lord Scalethorpe's got them where he wants them. And, if there ever are any suspicions about what's been going on, he can point to them as the culprits. Yes," Michael Bettleton said with reluctant admiration, "it's clever. That's why all the actual thefts have taken place while Lord Scalethorpe's out of the country. So that he'll never be suspected."

"But surely," objected Emma, "if Parkin does get arrested before they've completed the plan and he's escaped abroad, all he has to do is tell the police that Lord Scalethorpe's behind it."

"Yes, but would he be believed? Lord Scalethorpe's no fool. I bet he's set this up so that there is absolutely no proof of his involvement, nothing written down. So, if it did come to a confrontation, it'd just be Parkin's word against Lord Scalethorpe's. And who do you think the police are more likely to believe—a suspected criminal or a peer of the realm?"

"I see what you mean."

"It'd sound as if Kevin Parkin was trying to save his

131

own skin by accusing his employer. No one would believe it."

Michael Bettleton paused; then an expression of annoyance crossed his face. "Oh, it's frustrating! This is just the sort of case I like—I mean, exposing villains."

"It's the kind of thing you've done on lots of your television programs."

"Exactly, Emma. But this one's difficult. I always have to check all the facts incredibly carefully before I start making accusations, and in this case I just don't see how I'm going to get enough evidence. I mean, I'm fairly sure we're on the right track, but there's very little we can actually prove."

"We can prove that the armor's not the real stuff."

"Oh, yes. We can probably nail Parkin and his henchmen without too much problem. But I've still a nasty feeling Lord Scalethorpe himself will wriggle off our hook."

"Couldn't you set up a televised interview with him and confront him with the facts?" asked Stewie.

Michael Bettleton shook his head. "If I did that, it'd just set off warning bells, I'm sure. No, there must be another way. Oh, it's one of those occasions when I wish I could be on the spot with a television camera, have all the evidence at my fingertips, and really take someone totally by surprise."

"Do you know," said Emma, "I've thought of a way you could do exactly that."

✶ 22 ✶

Cheeky Charlie
Productions

Emma didn't get a chance to talk to her father until the following evening. Douglas Cobbett had been out on location Sunday and Monday and returned exhausted but satisfied because the two days of filming had gone well.

Experience had taught Emma to wait until her father was settled down with a large whiskey before questioning him, but on this occasion she didn't have time to get her request out. As soon as he saw her come into the room, Douglas said, "Oh, Emma, you know that production company you were asking me about?"

"Cheeky Charlie Productions."

"That's right. Well, I did find out something."

"Great."

"One of the actors I was working with today had been involved with them."

133

"They employed him?"

"Not exactly, no. In fact, the whole thing had left rather a nasty taste in his mouth. You see, he thought they'd employed him, but when it came down to it, they didn't have any money to pay him."

Emma looked puzzled and her father continued, "Cheeky Charlie Productions is a small company that was trying to set up a feature film . . . you know, a full-length film for the movies. Well, as you know from things I've said in the past, that is an extremely difficult business. Getting a script, getting a director, getting a cast—those are the easy parts. But raising the money is always a huge problem. Producers spend years going around begging from various financial institutions, and it can be pretty depressing work. One backer will agree to put in money only when they've raised half the budget, another will agree only when they've got a big list of other contributors, and so on and so on.

"The result is that film projects can be on and off for literally years. Everything's all set to start filming and one of the money men pulls out. Or everything's taken so long, and costs have gone up so much that the budget has to be doubled . . . all that kind of thing can go on.

"Anyway, it seems that Cheeky Charlie Productions was in this situation. They'd been trying to set up a big movie for ages, and eventually they seemed to have everything sorted out. There was a script, a director, locations in Mexico had been set up, they'd got a cast fixed—including the actor I was working with today. So, everyone went to Mexico, they did one and a half day's filming . . . and then suddenly everything went wrong."

"What happened?"

"I don't know the precise details, but basically the company just ran out of money. Maybe one of their big backers dropped out; maybe they just hadn't budgeted for enough. Anyway, the whole production collapsed, and the cast—many of whom had turned down other work to do the film—were left stranded in Mexico. They even had to pay their own fares back to England."

"But couldn't they have sued the company for compensation money?"

"No, it turned out that they'd never been properly contracted. The right legal papers hadn't been signed. The whole thing was a complete shambles and caused a lot of bad feeling."

"Hmm." Emma's brow furrowed as she thought about what she'd heard. "How long ago did this happen?"

"A couple of years ago."

"And so Cheeky Charlie Productions has gone out of business?"

"Well, the company still exists, but they certainly haven't made any films since that disaster."

"Do you know what the film was that they were setting up?"

"Sort of. I think that's why they came unstuck. It was a historical script, and those are always amazingly expensive for costumes and what-have-you."

"I bet it was set in the Middle Ages," said Emma.

Her father's eyebrows shot up in surprise. "How on earth do you know that?"

"Set in the Middle Ages, with lots of knights in armor," Emma continued.

"Yes. As it happens, you're right."

He looked at his daughter quizzically, but Emma didn't offer any explanation of her sudden knowledge. Instead, she asked, "Daddy, on a big production like that, what would happen with the costumes and stuff? How would they get out to the location?"

"Well, it varies from production to production. Sometimes the costumes will be made locally. Sometimes— particularly if it's specialist stuff—it'll be made here and shipped out."

"And armor would be specialist stuff, wouldn't it?"

"I'd say so, yes. Usually, anyway."

"And the stuff that got shipped out wouldn't have any problem getting through customs?"

"Well, no. I mean, obviously it would be checked, like anything else. But the customs officers would have been told what was coming and what it was for, and I don't see why there should be any problems."

"And customs officers wouldn't be surprised if costumes were still being shipped out for a film that was no longer being made?"

Douglas Cobbett looked more puzzled than ever. "They could hardly be expected to know about film schedules, could they? So long as the paperwork was okay, they wouldn't worry. But why should anyone ship out costumes for a nonexistent film? What is all this, Emma?"

"I really can't explain at the moment, Daddy. I will when it's all sorted out. I promise."

And her father had to be content with that for the time being.

Emma immediately phoned Michael Bettleton and told him what she had discovered. He was impressed.

"Yes, I like the sound of that. They get the replica suits of armor made by some theatrical armorer, who genuinely thinks they're for a film that's in production. Then they swap the suits for the real ones at Scalethorpe Castle.

"The real armor then gets shipped out to Mexico under the replica armor's paperwork and gets through customs with no problem. I mean, customs officers aren't going to be experts, are they? The paperwork says the crates contain replica armor. If they look inside, sure enough, what they see is armor. They're not to know whether it's the real stuff or not. And, they're certainly not to know whether Cheeky Charlie Productions is still in business or not."

"That's right. Then the armor's delivered to some contact in Mexico, who arranges the sale."

"Exactly, Emma. You have to admit it's clever. Hmm, this is a really useful lead. I'm going to follow it up. I think I might go to Mexico for a few days."

"But, Michael, that's going to cost you a bundle."

"Don't worry. This is such a big story, once I've got the proof, I'll have all the television companies and newspapers in the country falling over each other to buy it from me."

"Well, if you're sure it's going to be worth it . . ."

"You bet it will be. I'll get a flight tomorrow morning. Then maybe I'll be able to find some proof that Lord Scalethorpe himself is involved. He went to the States recently, didn't he?"

"Yes. Trying to raise American money to help keep British art treasures in this country," said Emma sarcastically.

"Oh, the hypocrite! I'd love to nail him for this. You know, it's a story that gets better and better by the minute. Perhaps I'll be able to prove that he went down to Mexico during his trip . . . or that he met up with someone involved with the Mexican end of the operation . . ."

"Well, good luck."

"Thanks. Oh, by the way, Emma, did you ask your father about the other business?"

"Sorry, I completely forgot once he started on Cheeky Charlie Productions. But look, don't worry, I'll ask him right away. If you don't hear from me, assume it's okay."

"Right. Thanks. You know, Emma," said Michael Bettleton before he put the phone down, "you'd make a great investigative reporter. You've got all the right instincts."

                    *   *   *

"OOPS!" echoed Douglas Cobbett, scarcely able to believe his ears. "You actually want to go and see them making *OOPS!*"

"Yes."

"But, Emma, I wouldn't have thought that was your sort of program at all. It's awful."

"I know, but we really would like to see one. If you can arrange it . . ."

"Oh, I can arrange it, all right. I'm just surprised, that's all. I don't know how many more there are in the series, but—"

"It's the last of the series we want. The live one. The one they're holding at Scalethorpe Castle."

"Oh, yes, I've heard about that. All the audience have to dress up in medieval costume for it."

"That's fine. Leave the costume to us. If you could just arrange the tickets."

Douglas Cobbett still looked bewildered as he said, "Sure. Yes. No problem. How many do you want?"

"Four," Emma replied firmly.

✤ 23 ✤

Oops! Again

It was a good thing that medieval dress was required for the audience of the last *OOPS!* of the series, because that enabled the Three Detectives to disguise themselves easily. After their earlier adventures in Scalethorpe Castle, they had no desire to be recognized by Kevin Parkin or his henchmen.

Emma wore a long red gown and had fixed a false blond fringe over her forehead; it was held in position by the tight linen bands that framed her face. Marcus and Stewie were dressed in brightly colored tunics and tights, and they had obscured their faces with baggy hoods.

Michael Bettleton was disguised by a false beard and wore knitted chain-mail under a crusader's long white tunic with a red cross on it.

The rest of the audience wore medieval costumes in varying degrees of authenticity, and all seemed very excited as the beginning of the program approached.

They were going to start in the banqueting hall. Fewer tables had been laid out than would be for one of the castle's regular medieval banquets; this was to make room for the large cameras on their wheeled pedestals to move around the room. Monitor screens, looking just like ordinary television sets, were positioned around the room, so that the audience would be able to see the pictures that were being transmitted to the viewing audience.

There was a High Table, at which Chris Chitty and the other *OOPS!* hosts were to sit, along with the fat Lord of the Revels and his apologetic-looking handmaidens. Stewie touched Marcus's arm and pointed at some other people who were joining the High Table: Kevin Parkin, Don, and Stan, all resplendent in medieval court dress. And, limping along to join them in a heavy purple brocade gown with fur trimmings was Lord Scalethorpe himself.

Stewie and Marcus glanced across at Michael Bettleton. Under his false beard, his face was tanned from the recent trip to Mexico. When he saw the arrival of Lord Scalethorpe, he looked grimly satisfied and beckoned one of the waiting cameramen over to him for a whispered conference. The man handed him something, which the reporter clipped to his tunic. Emma recognized it as a radio-microphone.

141

The program was set up as if during a banquet, and the audience was served by wenches in low-cut blouses with wooden dishes, on which were placed a chicken leg and a bowl of a thick yellow porridge-like substance.

"What's that?" asked Stewie curiously, as his was put in front of him.

"Frumenty," said the serving wench.

"I beg your pardon?"

"Frumenty."

"What's that?"

"I don't know. That's what it's called. I just serve it. Don't know what it's made of, but it's supposed to be medieval. All I know is that it comes in a packet and they mix it up with water in the kitchens."

"Yuk," said Stewie.

Then the wench slammed down a metal cup full of some pale, sticky-looking substance. Stewie sniffed it. It smelled horribly sweet.

"And what's that?" he asked.

"Mead," said the wench. "Fermented honey."

"Yuk," said Stewie again.

But then his attention was drawn by the producer of *OOPS!* clapping his hands for silence. "Look now, everyone, we're going to be on the air live in a few minutes. Just a couple of points for the audience. One, please don't eat all your food and drink all your drink too quickly. If the camera comes on you, we want to see you munching away. Okay? And, two, for heaven's sake, *smile* all the time. Got that? *OOPS!* is a happy show, remember, and the audience at home wants to see that everyone's having a wonderful time. Okay?

"So, once the custard pies start flying about, make sure you laugh and clap. Okay? There are millions of people out there watching tonight, and they all want to see how much you're enjoying yourselves.

"And, remember, *OOPS!* is a show where anything can happen. So be ready—you're going to have a few surprises this evening!"

"You can say that again," Emma murmured.

The show started and was pretty predictable. Chris Chitty and his assistants went through an exaggerated version of a medieval banquet, picking out carefully selected members of the public to be abused and have custard pies thrown at them, while they kept fixed smiles on their faces and demonstrated what "good sports" they were.

The medieval audience thought it was hilarious and roared with laughter and clapped and did all the idiotic, mindless things that the producer had wanted them to.

Michael Bettleton and the Three Detectives joined in, so as not to draw attention to themselves, and bided their time.

The show reached its first commercial break and there was some hasty repositioning of cameras before the next part of the program. The producer once again addressed his audience. "Now this part of the show's going to be the *OOPS!* awards. You know, the ones we've been building up to through the series—Idiot of the Year, Best Trip-up of the Year, Most Embarrassing Mistake by a Television Announcer, all that. So we want heaps of cheering and applause for the winners. Okay? And heaps when Lord Scalethorpe's introduced. He's going to give the awards, you see. And don't forget—be ready for all those surprises!"

Emma looked from under her blond fringe at Michael Bettleton. He smiled grimly and nodded. The moment was drawing near.

The second part of the program started with a compilation of clips from various filmed disasters that had been featured through the series. There were cars bumping into each other, people tripping, falling into water, being hit by custard pies—generally, as ever, being made to look like idiots.

The audience watched on the monitors, cheering and applauding every clip.

"Well, there they were," said Chris Chitty heartily. "Just a few highlights from the last series of *OOPS!* And some of those may feature in the list of award-winners, because now it's time to find out who are the biggest twits we've seen over the last few weeks! Yes, it's time for the *OOPS!* awards, including that most prestigious of all awards—Idiot of the Year!"

The audience roared their appreciation of this prospect.

"And, to present our awards, we are very honored to have with us someone who really raises the class of this program no end. Yes, a genuine member of the British aristocracy—the owner of this magnificent castle where we have the honor to be tonight. Will you put your hands together, please, and welcome—Lord Scalethorpe!"

The audience did as they were requested and gave the noble lord a tremendous welcome.

Lord Scalethorpe stood up with the assured smile of a practiced public speaker. "Thank you very much. And may I say that the honor you speak of goes both ways. You may feel honored to be here, but I also feel honored to be host to such a splendid program as *OOPS!* It's wonderful to see the twentieth century and the Middle Ages coming together in such a jolly way!

"Because, you know, *OOPS!* is a program that appeals to us all. All of us enjoy seeing other people make mistakes. And, you know, all of us should be able to see the funny side of the mistakes we make ourselves." He gave a rueful grin. "Because we've all made mistakes, haven't we? You know, I'm not ashamed to admit it— even I've made mistakes in my time—"

"Yes, you have, haven't you!"

The new voice took everyone by surprise. Emma glanced up at the monitor screen and saw Michael Bettleton, in his crusader's uniform, framed beside Lord Scalethorpe. Good, the cameraman was doing his stuff. The noble lord was being confronted with his crime in front of millions of live television viewers.

While everyone gaped in shock, the reporter whipped off his false beard and announced, "I am Michael Bettleton, and I have proof that you, Lord Scalethorpe, have been secretly selling off the armor collection of Scalethorpe Castle!"

"What?" the noble lord mouthed helplessly.

"You have been substituting replica armor for the real stuff, which you have been exporting to Mexico in the name of a film company called Cheeky Charlie Productions." He flourished some typewritten sheets from inside his tunic. "I have here written statements from your Mexican contact, who was responsible for selling the armor abroad. He confesses his own part in the crime and also has proof of your involvement, Lord Scalethorpe."

"I don't believe it," Lord Scalethorpe murmured.

"It's true," Michael Bettleton continued implacably. "Your contact, who has made these statements in front of a lawyer, is Diego Henriques!"

The mention of this name had an effect like an electric shock on Lord Scalethorpe's face. Guilt was clearly written across it. But he was a cool operator and might still have recovered himself and bluffed his way out of the accusation.

His partners-in-crime, however, had not such strong nerves.

"We've got to get out of here!" shouted Kevin Parkin, rising to his feet, along with Stan and Don. As they did so, the two bigger men gave the High Table a great push, which overturned it in a confusion of dishes and goblets.

The three crooks turned toward the door and found their way barred by Chris Chitty. On his face was a strange expression; he didn't know whether all this was part of the show or not. So he kept his fixed smile to show what a wonderful time he was having, but he managed at the same time to look very cross that people were doing things they hadn't told him about. He made a living out of springing surprises on other people and expecting them to be "good sports"; when he was the victim of a surprise, he seemed unable to see the funny side. "What's going on?" he demanded.

"Oh, get out of the way!" Stan roared, and, to the huge delight of the audience, upturned a jug of sticky mead over the unfortunate host.

The crooks' next obstacle was the fat Lord of the Revels, who was pushed out of the way with a dish of gooey frumenty in his face.

The audience thought this was wonderful. As the producer had requested that they should, they roared and clapped. Then, thinking perhaps that they should join in the fun, they started hurling their own dishes of frumenty and cups of mead around. The air was full of flying missiles, many of which landed with satisfying splats on other members of the audience. The people who were hit grinned inanely to show what "good sports" they were.

The cameramen weaved back and forth, catching all the action they could. It was one of the liveliest editions of *OOPS!* that anyone could remember, but in all the confusion Kevin Parkin and his crew managed to escape.

Lord Scalethorpe also decided that he'd better get away. Stewie just caught a glimpse, through the hail of frumenty, of the purple brocade robe disappearing through the banqueting hall's huge double doors.

"Quick!" he shouted to the other two detectives. "After them!"

⚜ 24 ⚜
The Ghost

The banqueting hall was the other side of the castle from the armory. Had the escaping criminals gone out by a different door, they would have been near the back entrance, but it seemed clear from the direction they were taking that they were making for the main gatehouse.

The Three Detectives could hear the clump of feet ahead of them, as they rushed along the stone passages. Even Lord Scalethorpe, in spite of his limp, seemed to be moving very quickly.

Stewie led the pursuers, getting farther and farther ahead of Emma, and Marcus, whose weight always slowed him down, puffed along behind. Michael Bettleton seemed still to be involved in the banqueting hall. There was no sound of his following them.

Stewie pounded up a spiral staircase. He wasn't really

thinking about where he was or what he'd do if he caught up with the villains. His only thought was to overtake them. Then he'd think of something.

He heard a door thump shut above him and tried to go even faster up the winding stone stairs. Then he was on a small landing, and he found himself faced with a heavy studded wooden door. He grasped the latch, turned it, and pushed through.

It was suddenly dark and cold. Through the windows he could see what a gloomy, lowering night it was, a night on which weak moonbeams washed everything with an unearthly pallor.

It was only then that Stewie realized that he was in the long gallery. And only then he saw, walking toward him, glowing slightly in the thin, deceptive light, the armored figure of Sir Roger Scalethorpe.

For a moment he was immobilized. He felt his will drain from him, as a cold sweat burst out all over his body. The nightmare that had been haunting him for weeks had at last become reality.

But he had to fight it. He had to explode the fear himself. No one else could help him. It was just Stewart Hinde, alone, face to face with his own fear and superstition.

He took a deep breath, then, rushing forward with a cry of "There are no ghosts!", launched himself at the shadowy figure ahead.

He half expected to float through the outline, to find that the suit of armor had no substance, that he was clutching at nothingness.

But no. What he grasped was very solid. Not only solid, but very much alive and kicking. The figure fought back fiercely against his grip.

Stewie wrestled, scrabbling for a handhold on the slippery surface of the armor. Meanwhile the armed feet kicked away at his shins, trying to throw him off his balance.

Stewie fought back, pressing to get a leg behind the armored figure, struggling to topple his mysterious opponent.

For a second the knight in armor's struggles seemed to grow weaker. Stewie took advantage and, slipping a leg behind, pushed with all his strength.

At first the knight did not seem to move. Then, slowly, he lost his balance and crashed to the ground with a dull rattle of armor.

At that moment light flooded the long gallery, and Stewie looked back to see Emma at the door with her hand on the switch.

He knelt down beside the figure on the floor. It moved slightly, suggesting that it was not too badly hurt. Stewie raised the visor of the fiberglass helmet and looked down into the dazed eyes of the weasel-faced squire, Keith.

✣ 25 ✣

The Battle
of Scalethorpe Armory

From the long gallery, Lord Scalethorpe and his gang had to go through the armory to get to the castle's main gate, and this delayed them. Afraid of curious eyes inspecting the exhibits when there were so many people around the castle, Kevin Parkin had decided that the armory should be locked at both ends, and it took a minute or two for them to open the first set of doors.

But they were inside by the time Stewie got to the door. He hid behind it and peered around. The only light came from the faint glow of the EXIT signs.

"Should we have locked it again to keep them out?" asked Kevin Parkin's voice from the space ahead.

"Don't worry. Young Keith'll keep them quiet for a bit," said Lord Scalethorpe's voice. He laughed harshly. "The ghost once again guarding the castle's treasures."

"I hope so." A jangle of keys accompanied Kevin Parkin's voice. "There are three locks to do on this one."

Stewie heard a slight panting behind him and turned to see Emma approaching. He put his fingers to his lips and indicated that they should slip into the armory.

Silent on soft shoes, they crept down the steps, keeping their bodies close to the walls. "Got to stop them getting out," Stewie breathed. "Let's go and get some weapons."

They slipped across to a display of swords and pikes, dimly outlined in the feeble light. Ahead they could hear the jangle of keys and muttered curses as Kevin Parkin tried to find the keyholes in the dimness.

Hastily, Stewie picked up a pointed Spanish helmet, a shield, and a short sword. Emma selected a heavy mace and a round shield.

"Right," Stewie murmured. "Let's try them with a bit of their own medicine."

He saw Emma nod in the gloom, then, banging their weapons against nearby suits of armor, the two detectives leaped out of the darkness into the dimly lit center of the armory.

The group by the door turned and froze in horror at the sight of the two shadowy armed figures approaching them. There was a clatter as Kevin Parkin's bunch of keys fell to the floor.

"Blimey!" whispered Stan. "Ghosts!"

"Yeah," said Don in a trembly voice. "We shouldn't have never got messed up in all this!"

153

Lord Scalethorpe's voice rose above theirs. "Don't be ridiculous! We know what those two are up to. We've used the same methods ourselves. Those aren't ghosts—it's those wretched kids again!"

"Oh, yeah, so it is."

Don and Stan looked angry and ugly as they both took long-handled axes down from the walls. Lord Scalethorpe reached for a huge two-handed sword.

"Get that door open, Parkin!" he hissed. "Meanwhile we're going to give these two a lesson they won't forget in a hurry!"

The three men advanced toward the two detectives, weighing their weapons in their hands.

Emma dodged behind a tall suit of armor. Don took a swing, and his axe bit into the armor sending the whole display clattering to the ground and exposing her once again to danger. Emma ducked behind another huge suit.

Stan was meanwhile approaching Stewie, twirling his great axe as if it were as light as a tennis racket. Stewie ducked and felt the wind of the blade whistling over his head.

He grabbed a long spear from the wall and held it out to keep his attacker at bay. Stan took another swing, sliced through the lance, and left Stewie holding a two-foot wooden stump in his hands.

The boy threw it, but the man brushed the missile aside with his arm and continued to advance. Stewie looked around and saw that he was being backed into a corner. He looked up to the dim outline of a spray of swords and lances clustered behind a round shield on the wall. He reached upward.

The second suit of armor behind which Emma crouched was more solid than the first one. Don's axe smashed through the metal of its breastplate and got stuck into the wooden frame underneath. The man swore and wrestled to free the deeply embedded blade.

Peering upward, Emma saw the huge outline of the armor shake and shift as he tried to get the axe out. She waited till it leaned away from her, then, taking a deep breath, gave it a firm shove just above the waist.

She was rewarded by the sight of the figure falling away, and a slight scream from Don as it crashed in a jangle of metal on top of him.

Stewie pulled at the shaft of the lance on the wall above him. It stayed firm. He couldn't shift it. Stan continued to come closer. In the dim light, Stewie could see an ugly smile forming on the man's lips. The boy reached up-ward and, as the axe was swung, heaved himself up on the shaft.

It worked. The axe struck sparks off the stone just be-low his feet.

Stan straightened himself, preparing for another blow.

At that moment, with horror, Stewie felt something above him give way. There was a metallic tearing sound.

His weight had been too much for the display of weapons on the wall.

He felt himself dropping and, very slowly, saw the huge star-shape of swords and lances detach itself from the wall and fall down in a great arc.

The round shield at the center of the display landed squarely on Stan's head, and he crumpled to the ground in a clanging of metal.

"You little monsters! You've ruined everything!"

It was Lord Scalethorpe's voice, but the sound was almost unrecognizable. Gone were the measured, cool tones of the politician; all control was lost, and the voice had risen to a scream of fury.

Suddenly there was light in the armory. Kevin Parkin had opened the other doors, but all they revealed was a row of policemen standing waiting for him. He turned back in horror.

Then there was more light. The switch was thrown at the other end of the armory, revealing Marcus and Michael Bettleton, along with many of the *OOPS!* production team.

On the floor Don and Stan sat dazed, foolishly rubbing their heads.

But the sudden light didn't stop Lord Scalethorpe. He continued speeding across the stone slabs, whirling the great warsword above his head as one of his ancestors might have done six hundred years before. His eyes were wild as he stormed toward Stewie, who crouched, winded, on the floor.

"Stop!"

"Don't make it worse!"

"Don't hurt him!"

But Lord Scalethorpe did not seem to hear the cries from the doorways. He was so furious that he heard nothing.

Instead, he swung the mighty sword and brought it down with all his force on Stewie's head.

Everyone in the room was silent at the impact. Then they heard the clatter of the broken pieces of sword falling to the floor.

Stewie grinned at his attacker and tapped the helmet on his head. "I got a real one, Lord Scalethorpe. Built to protect, you know. Those armorers really knew what they were doing in those days."

The noble lord gaped as he looked at the broken hilt of the sword he still clutched in his hand. Its hollowness was exposed for all to see.

"You weren't so lucky, though, were you, Lord Scalethorpe? Caught by your own little plot, I'm afraid." Stewie pointed to the remains of the sword and laughed. "You got a fiberglass one."

❧ 26 ❧

No More Knights
in Armor

"So you really mean," said Emma in disbelief, "that Lord Scalethorpe is going to get off scot-free?"

Michael Bettleton gave a wry smile. "Well, not quite scot-free. I mean, he's having to sell Scalethorpe Castle, which is what he was trying to avoid doing in the first place. And I've a feeling that, after his exposure on television, he will probably spend most of the rest of his life living abroad."

"He won't go to prison, though?"

Michael Bettleton shook his head. "I very much doubt it."

"But Kevin Parkin and Stan and Don have all been sent to prison."

"Yes, but they haven't got the kind of lawyers Lord Scalethorpe has. It's quite a business to imprison a peer of the realm, you know."

"But there's so much evidence against him. I mean, apart from the theft of the armor, there were lots of witnesses to his attack on Stewie. Even the police saw it, for goodness' sake!"

"I've still got a feeling Lord Scalethorpe won't be prosecuted," said Michael Bettleton wryly.

"But . . . but . . . but . . ." Emma was speechless with anger.

"Incidentally," asked Marcus, "how did the police come to be there? Had you set them up?"

The reporter nodded. "Yes, I gave them a call. I had plenty of evidence to get Kevin and his two thugs arrested, so I asked the police to come to the castle."

"You have evidence against Lord Scalethorpe, too," Emma protested.

"Oh, yes. But, as I say, I somehow don't think any charges will be brought against him."

"Huh," said Emma. "Well, I think it's disgusting. He planned the whole thing, he was really the one manipulating the others, and he gets away with it. It's not fair!"

"I'm afraid a lot of things that happen aren't fair." The reporter swirled his beer around in the glass. "And I'm afraid it's the Lord Scalethorpes of this life who tend always to land on their feet."

"And what'll happen to the castle?"

"I think that could be good news, actually. Some good coming out of all this. Scalethorpe Castle's likely to be bought by some kind of trust, so it'll still be open to the public."

"Oh, well, that's something."

There was a silence. "More to drink?" asked Marcus. They were up in his den, and he took his duty as host seriously. Michael Bettleton shook his head.

"Something more to eat?" Marcus indicated the tray of cakes that Birgit had prepared, but again Michael declined the offer.

"No, really. I must be off soon. I've got to interview some people tonight."

"Another investigation under way? About to expose more criminals?"

He nodded.

"I wish we could say the same," complained Stewie. "Life's been really dull since the end of the Scalethorpe Castle case."

"Something else'll turn up."

"Hmm. Hope you're right."

"How's Gary?" asked Emma. "Have you heard from him recently?"

"Spoke to him last week. He's fine. Made a full recovery."

"Has he got any acting work? I gave him my father's name. Daddy's always willing to meet actors and try and help them when he's got suitable parts in shows he's doing. But he said he hasn't heard anything from Gary."

Again Michael Bettleton shook his head. "No, he wouldn't have. Gary's decided to give up acting."

"Really?"

"Yes. All that time in the hospital gave him a chance

to think about what he really wanted to do. And he decided it wasn't show business. He's never had the right temperament to cope with all that insecurity, all those long periods with no work."

"So what's he going to do instead?"

"Well, the one bit of the Scalethorpe Castle job he really enjoyed was the riding . . . you know, for the jousting. He's always loved horses, and now he's got a job working for a local stables. He's as happy as can be."

"That's great."

There was another silence. Somehow everyone felt flat. They had been looking forward to this meeting with Michael Bettleton, a chance to talk about the case and tie up the loose ends, but now that it had happened, it all seemed a bit of an anticlimax.

"One thing I've never really understood," said the reporter, "is how this thing started. I mean, you said you first got interested in the case when Stewie met a knight in armor in the woods."

"Yes, that's right. Well, obviously, that knight in armor was Keith . . ."

"Hmm."

"Who, incidentally, it turns out, is Kevin Parkin's son."

"Oh, that makes sense. There's quite a likeness when you think about it."

"Yes. Well, apparently," said Stewie, "that tilting armor of Sir Roger Scalethorpe's was one of the first ones they substituted, and when they saw how small and light it was, they had the idea of putting Keith in it to build up the stories about the Scalethorpe Castle ghost. They got him to walk along the long gallery a few moonlit nights, reckoning that it would only take a couple of sightings to get the story going . . ."

"Which was partly just for publicity," said Marcus. "As we thought . . ."

"And partly to keep snoopers away from the castle at nighttime. It was quite a clever way of ensuring that they wouldn't be disturbed while they were substituting the armor."

"Except by the Three Detectives," Michael chuckled.

"Right."

"I see all that. But what I don't see is why Keith was wandering around in his suit of armor in the middle of a Thursday afternoon."

Stewie grinned. "Actually, I asked him that."

"What, you've seen him since?"

"Yes. I've got to know him quite well. Now he's away from his father's influence, he's really quite nice. Very keen on history and armor and all that sort of stuff."

"Is he? That's good to hear. All right then, Stewie, why was he wandering about in armor on a Thursday afternoon?"

"You know he helped with the tournaments?"

"Yes."

"Well, he was desperately keen to do some of the actual jousting, but his father wouldn't let him, so he was teaching himself secretly. He'd borrow a horse from the stables, take a lance, and go off and practice. Well, once he got that suit of fiberglass tilting armor, he couldn't resist having a go with that."

"Which is what he was doing that afternoon you saw him?"

"What he had been doing, yes. In a field near the castle. But he'd just been thrown by his horse, which had bolted. When I saw him that afternoon, he was simply looking for his horse."

"Goodness," said Emma, "if you'd known that from the start, it would've saved you a few worries, wouldn't it, Stewie?"

"Yes. On the other hand, if I'd known that from the start, we'd never have investigated the case, would we?" And he grinned in a way that suggested a few worries were a small price to pay for the excitements of an investigation with the Three Detectives.

Michael Bettleton left soon after, and the Three Detectives also prepared to go their separate ways.

Marcus was keen to get on with a new computer program he had devised for creating an unbreakable code. Emma had arranged to play tennis with a friend. And Stewie had to go back home to do his history homework. Ugh. Yet another of Mr. Hendricks's inspiring essay subjects: "The Development of the British Iron and Steel Industries during the Second Half of the Eighteenth Century."

Huh, thought Stewie as he pressed down hard on the pedals of his old rattletrap of a bicycle, that's not history.

And his mind filled with a glowing vision of himself, Sir Stewart Hinde, dressed in full tilting armor, mounted on a huge horse and galloping with his lance at the ready toward another brave knight in a tournament.